Inseparable

Inseparable

A NEVER-BEFORE-PUBLISHED NOVEL

SIMONE DE BEAUVOIR

TRANSLATED FROM THE FRENCH BY SANDRA SMITH

An Imprint of HarperCollins*Publishers*

HarperCollins books may be purchased for educational, business, or sales promotional use. For information, please email the Special Markets Department at SPsales@harpercollins.com.

Ecco® and HarperCollins® are trademarks of HarperCollins Publishers.

Originally published as *Les inséparables* in France in 2020 by Éditions de L'Herne.

FIRST U.S. EDITION

Designed by Michelle Crowe

Library of Congress Cataloging-in-Publication Data has been applied for.

ISBN 978-0-06-307504-7

21 22 23 24 25 LSC 10 9 8 7 6 5 4 3 2 1

TO ZAZA

If I have tears in my eyes tonight, is it because you have died, or rather because I'm the one who is still alive? I should dedicate this story to you: but I know that you are nowhere now, and that I am speaking to you here through literary artfulness. Besides, this is not truly your story but simply a story inspired by us. You were not Andrée and I am not the Sylvie who speaks in my name.

CONTENTS

INTRODUCTION

BY MARGARET ATWOOD

How exciting to learn that Simone de Beauvoir, grandmother of second-wave feminism, had written a novel that had never been published! In French it was called *Les inséparables* and was said by the journal *Les libraires* to be a story that "follows with emotion and clarity the passionate friendship between two rebellious young women." Of course I wanted to read it, but then I was asked to write an introduction to the English translation.

My initial reaction was panic. This was a throwback: as a young person, I was terrified of Simone de Beauvoir. I went to university at the end of the fifties and the beginning of the sixties, when, among the black-turtleneck-wearing, heavily eyelinered cognoscenti—admittedly not numerous in the Toronto of those days—the French Existentialists were worshipped as minor gods. Camus, how revered! How eagerly we read his grim novels! Beckett, how adored! His plays, especially *Waiting for Godot*, were favorites of college drama clubs. Ionesco and the Theatre of the Absurd, how puzzling! Yet his plays, too, were often performed among us (and some, such as *Rhinoceros*—a metaphor for fascist takeovers—are increasingly pertinent). Sartre, how bafflingly smart, though not what you'd call cute. Who hadn't quoted "Hell is other people"? (Did we recognize that the corollary would have to be "Heaven is solitude"? No, we did not. Did we forgive him for having sucked up to Stalinism for so many years? Yes, we did, more or less, because he'd denounced the invasion of Hungary by the U.S.S.R. in 1956, then had written an incandescent introduction to Henri Alleg's *The Question* (1958), an account of Alleg's brutal torture at the hands of the French military during the Algerian war—a book banned in France by the government but available to us in the boonies, as I read it in 1961.)

But among all these intimidating Existentialist luminaries there was only one female person: Simone de Beauvoir. How frighteningly tough she must be, I thought, to be holding her own among the super-intellectual steely brained Parisian Olympians! It was a time when women who aspired to be more than embodiments of assigned gender roles felt they had to comport themselves like macho men—coldly, with avowed self-interest—while seizing the initiative, even the sexual initiative. A bon mot here, a slapping away of a wandering hand there, an insouciant affair, or two, or twenty, followed by cigarettes, as in films . . . I never would have been up to it, struggling as I was with the lesser demands of the college debating club. In addition to which, smoking made me cough. As for those dowdy wartime suits with the durability and the shoulder pads, those would have been far too high a price to pay for a room of one's own.

Why was Simone de Beauvoir so frightening to me? Easy for you to ask: you have the benefit of distance—dead people are less innately scary than living ones, especially if they've been cut down to size by biographers, ever alert to flaws—whereas for me, Beauvoir was a giant contemporary. There was the twenty-year-old me in provincial Toronto, dreaming of running away to Paris to compose masterpieces in a garret while working as a waitress, and there were the Existentialists, holding court at Le Dôme Café in Montparnasse, writing for *Les temps modernes*, and sneering at the likes of mousy me. I could imagine what they might say. *"Bourgeoise,"* they would begin, flicking the ashes off their Gitanes. Worse: Canadian. *"Quelques arpents de neige,"* they would quote Voltaire. Moreover, a Canadian from the backwoods. And the worst kind of backwoods Canadian: an Anglo. The dismissive contempt! The sophisticated disdain! There is no snobbism quite like French snobbism, especially that of the Left. (The Left of the mid-twentieth century, that is; I am sure no such thing would happen now.)

But then I grew somewhat older, and I actually went to Paris, where I was not rejected by Existentialists—I couldn't find any, as I couldn't afford to eat in Parisian cafés—and shortly after that I was in Vancouver, where I finally read *The Second Sex* from cover to cover, in the washroom so no one would see me doing it. (The year was 1964, and second-wave feminism had not yet arrived in the hinterlands of North America.)

At this point, some of my terror was replaced by pity. What a strict upbringing had been imposed upon the young Simone. How constrained she had felt, in her supervised body and frilly girl's clothing and rigidly prescribed social behavior. It seemed that there were advantages to being a backwoods Canadian girl after all: free from censorious nuns and demanding sets of highish-society relatives, I could run around in trousers—better than skirts, considering the mosquitoes—and paddle my own canoe and, once in high school, attend sock hops and go rollicking off to drive-in movies with slightly disreputable boyfriends. Such unconstrained and indeed unladylike comportment never would have been permitted to the young Simone. The strictness was for her own good, or so she would have been told. If she violated the rules of her class, ruin would await her, and disgrace would be the lot of her family.

It's worth reminding ourselves that France did not grant the vote to women until 1944, and then only through a law signed by Charles de Gaulle in exile. That's almost twenty-five years after most Canadian women gained the same right. So Beauvoir grew up hearing that women, in effect, were unworthy of having a say in the public life of the nation. She would have been thirty-six before she could vote, and then only in theory, since the Germans were still in control of France at that time.

Once she came of age, during the twenties, Simone de Beauvoir reacted strongly against her corseted background. I, being much less corseted, did not feel that the conditions described in *The Second Sex* applied to all women. Some of the book rang true to me, to be sure. Though by no means all of it.

In addition, there was the generation gap: I was born in 1939, whereas Beauvoir was born in 1908, a year before my mother. They were of the same cohort, though worlds apart. My mother grew up in rural Nova Scotia, where she was a tomboy, a horseback rider, and a speed skater. (Try to picture Simone de Beauvoir speed skating and you will grasp the difference.) Both had lived through World War I as children and World War II as adults, though France was at the center of both, and Canada—

though its wartime military losses were greatly out of pro-portion to its population—was never bombed and never occupied. The hardness, the flintiness, the unflinching stare at the uglier sides of existence that we find in Beauvoir are not unconnected to France's ordeals. Enduring these two wars, with their privations, dangers, anxieties, political in-fighting, and betrayals: that passage through hell would have taken its toll.

Thus my mother lacked the flinty gaze, having in-stead a cheerful, roll-up-your-sleeves, don't-whine prac-ticality that would have seemed offensively naive to any mid-century Parisian. Overcome by the oppressiveness of existence? Faced with a large rock that Sisyphus must roll uphill, only to have it roll down again? Plagued by the existential tension between justice and freedom? Striving for inner authenticity or, indeed, for meaning? Worried by how many men you'd have to sleep with in order to wipe the stain of the haute bourgeoisie from yourself forever? "Take a nice brisk walk in the fresh air," my mother would have said, "and you'll feel a lot better." When I was waxing too depressingly intellectual and/or morose, this was her advice to me.

My mother wouldn't have been very interested in the more abstract and philosophical portions of *The Second Sex*, but I expect she would have been intrigued by much of Simone de Beauvoir's other writing. From this distance it's arguable that Beauvoir's freshest and most immediate work comes directly from her own experience. Again and again she felt drawn back to her childhood, her youth, her young adulthood—exploring her own formation, her complex feelings, her sensations of the time. The best-known example is perhaps the first volume of her autobiography, *Mémoires d'une jeune fille rangée* (1958), but the same material appears in stories and novels. She was, in a sense, haunted by herself. Whose invisible but heavy footfall was that, coming inexorably up the dark stairway? It usually turned out to be hers. The ghost of her former self, or selves, was ever present.

And now we have a wellspring of sorts: *Inseparable*, unpublished until now. It recounts what was perhaps the single most influential experience of Beauvoir's life: her relationship with "Zaza"—the Andrée of the novel—a many-layered and intense friendship that ended with Zaza's early and tragic death.

Beauvoir wrote this book in 1954, five years after publishing *The Second Sex*, and made the mistake of showing it to Sartre. He judged most works by political standards and could not grasp its significance; for a materialist Marxist, this was odd, as the book is intensely descriptive of the physical and social conditions of its two young female characters. At that time the only means of production taken seriously had to do with factories and agriculture, not the unpaid and undervalued labor of women. Sartre dismissed this work as inconsequential. Beauvoir wrote of it in her memoir that it "seemed to have no inner necessity and failed to hold the reader's interest." This *appears* to have been a quote from Sartre, one with which Beauvoir *appears* to have agreed at the time.

Well, Dear Reader, Mr. "Hell is other people" Sartre was wrong, at least from this Dear Reader's perspective. I suppose that if you're keen on abstractions such as the Perfection of Humankind and Total Justice and Equality, you won't like novels much, since all novels are about individual people and their circumstances; and you particularly won't like novels written by your lady love about events that have taken place before you yourself have manifested in her life, and that feature an important, talented, and adored Other who happens to be female. The inner life of young girls of the bourgeoisie? How trivial. Pouf. Enough with this small-scale pathos, Simone. Turn your well-honed mind to more serious matters.

Ah, but M. Sartre, we reply from the twenty-first century, these *are* serious matters. Without Zaza, without the passionate devotion between the two of them, without Zaza's encouragement of Beauvoir's intellectual ambitions and her desire to break free of the conventions of her time, without Beauvoir's view of the crushing expectations placed on Zaza as a woman by her family and her society—

expectations that, in Beauvoir's view, literally squeezed the life out of her, despite her mind, her strength, her wit, her will—would there have been a *Second Sex*? And without that pivotal book, what else would not have followed?

Furthermore, how many versions of Zazas are living on the earth right now—bright, talented, capable women, some oppressed by the laws of their nations, others through poverty or discrimination within supposedly more gender-equal countries? *Inseparable* is particular to its own time and place—all novels are—but it transcends its own time and place as well.

Read it and weep, Dear Reader. The author herself weeps at the outset: this is how the story begins, with tears. It seems that, despite her forbidding exterior, Beauvoir never stopped weeping for the lost Zaza. Perhaps she herself worked so hard to become who she was as a sort of memorial: Beauvoir must express herself to the utmost, because Zaza could not.

CHAPTER 1

When I was nine, I was a very good girl; I hadn't always been. In my early childhood, the tyranny of adults threw me into such raging fits that one day, one of my aunts seriously declared: "Sylvie is possessed by demons." War and religion had defeated me. I immediately proved my exemplary patriotism by stomping on a plastic doll that was "made in Germany"; I didn't like it anyway. I was taught that my good behavior and piousness would determine whether God saved France: I couldn't escape. I walked through the Basilica of Sacré Coeur with the other little girls, waving banners and singing. I started praying a very great deal and grew to like it. Father Dominique, who was the chaplain at Adélaïde, my school, encouraged my devotion. Wearing a tulle dress and a bonnet made of Irish lace, I took my First Communion: from that day onward, I was held up as an example to my younger sisters.

My prayers were answered when my father was transferred to the War Ministry due to a heart condition.

On that particular morning, however, I was very excited; it was the first day of school. I was eager to get back: the classes (as solemn as a church Mass), the silence of the corridors, the sweet smiles of the young ladies. They wore long skirts and high-necked blouses, and since a part of the building had been transformed into a hospital, they often dressed as nurses. Beneath their white veils stained here and there with blood, they looked like saints, and I was moved when they pressed me to their hearts. I quickly wolfed down the soup and tasteless bread that had replaced the hot chocolate and brioche we'd had before the war, and waited impatiently as Mama finished dressing my sisters. All three of us had on sky blue coats made of the same fabric that the officers wore and tailored exactly like military greatcoats.

"Look, there's even a little belt!" said Mama to her admiring or amazed friends. As we left the building, Mama held hands with the two little ones. We sadly passed the Café de la Rotonde that had noisily opened below our apartment and which was, said Papa, a hideout for defeatists; the word intrigued me. "They are the people who believe in the defeat of France," Papa explained. "We should shoot them all." I didn't understand. You don't believe what you believe on purpose: could you be punished because certain ideas come into your mind? The spies who gave poisoned candy to children, or the ones who stabbed French women with poisoned needles, obviously deserved to die, but the defeatists left me perplexed. I didn't try to ask Mama: she always gave the same answers as Papa.

My little sisters did not walk quickly; the gates of the Luxembourg Gardens seemed to go on forever. Finally, I got to school, climbing up the stairs and happily swinging my schoolbag full of new books. I recognized the faint odor of sick patients mixed in with the smell of floor wax in the freshly polished hallways; the supervisors hugged me. In the coatroom, I saw my friends from the year before; I wasn't close with anyone in particular, but I liked the noise we made all together. I stood for a while in the large auditorium, in front of the display cases full of old dead things that managed to die a second time: stuffed birds lost their feathers, dried plants crumbled, shells faded. The bell rang and I went into the Sainte Marguerite classroom; all the classrooms were the same. The pupils sat around an oval table covered in black moleskin and were supervised by the teacher. Our mothers sat behind us, watching us as they knitted balaclavas. I headed to my seat and saw that the one next to mine was taken by a little girl I didn't know; she had brown hair and hollow cheeks and looked much younger than I was. Her dark, shining eyes stared at me intensely.

"Are you the best pupil?"

"I'm Sylvie Lepage," I said. "What's your name?"

"Andrée Gallard. I'm nine; if I look younger, it's because I was burnt to a crisp and didn't grow much. I couldn't go to school for a year, but Mama wants me to catch up. Could you lend me your notebooks from last year?"

"Yes," I said.

Andrée's confidence and her precise, rapid way of speaking unsettled me. She looked me up and down defiantly.

"The girl next to me said you were the best pupil," she said, nodding slightly toward Lisette. "Is it true?"

"I'm often at the top of the class," I said somewhat shyly.

I stared at Andrée; her dark hair fell straight down around her face, and she had an ink stain on her chin. You don't meet a little girl who was burned alive every day, so I wanted to ask her a lot of questions, but Mademoiselle Dubois had come in, her long dress sweeping across the floor. She was a brisk woman who had a mustache and whom I respected a lot. She sat down and called out our names; she looked up at Andrée: "Well, my dear, we don't feel too intimidated, do we?"

"I'm not shy, Mademoiselle," said Andrée confidently. "Besides," she added pleasantly, "you're not intimidating."

Mademoiselle Dubois hesitated for a moment, then

smiled beneath her mustache and continued taking attendance.

The end of classes finished with the usual ritual: Mademoiselle stood at the doorstep, shook the hand of each mother, and kissed every child on the forehead. She placed her hand on Andrée's shoulder: "You've never been to school?"

"No; until now I've worked at home, but now I'm too big."

"I hope you'll follow in your older sister's footsteps," said Mademoiselle.

"Oh! We're very different," said Andrée. "Malou takes after Papa, she loves math, but I especially love literature."

Lisette poked me with her elbow. You couldn't say that Andrée was impertinent, but she didn't use the tone of voice she should have when talking to a teacher.

"Do you know where the study room is for day students? If no one comes to pick you up right away, that's where you should go and wait," said Mademoiselle.

"No one is coming to pick me up; I'm going home by myself," said Andrée, then quickly added, "Mama told the school."

"By yourself?" asked Mademoiselle Dubois; Andrée shrugged. "Well, if your mother told the school . . ."

Mademoiselle Dubois kissed me on the forehead when it was my turn, and I followed Andrée into the coatroom.

She slipped on her coat: it was not as unique as mine, but it was very pretty, made of thick wool, red with gold buttons. She wasn't a street urchin, so why was she allowed to go out alone? Wasn't her mother aware of the danger of deadly candy and poisoned needles?

"Where do you live, Andrée dear?" asked Mama as we were going down the stairs with my little sisters.

"Rue de Grenelle."

"Oh, well, then! We'll walk with you to the Boulevard Saint-Germain," said Mama. "It's on our way."

"With pleasure," said Andrée, "but please don't go out of your way for me." She looked at Mama. "You see, Madame," she said quite seriously, "there are seven of us children; Mama says that we have to learn how to manage by ourselves."

Mama nodded, but it was obvious she didn't approve.

As soon as we were out on the street, I questioned Andrée: "How did you get burned?"

"I was cooking some potatoes over a campfire; my dress caught fire, and my right thigh was burned right down to the bone." Andrée made a small gesture of impatience; this old story bored her. "When can I see your notebooks? I need to know what you studied last year. Tell me where you live, and I'll come by this afternoon or tomorrow."

I looked at Mama for approval; I wasn't allowed to play with children I didn't know in the Luxembourg Gardens.

"This week isn't possible," said Mama, sounding embarrassed. "Maybe on Saturday; we'll see."

"All right; I'll wait until Saturday," said Andrée.

I watched her cross the wide boulevard in her red woolen coat; she was really very small, but she walked with the confidence of an adult.

"Your uncle Jacques knew the Gallards, who were related to the Lavergnes, the Blanchards' cousins," Mama said in a dreamy voice. "I wonder if it's the same family. But it seems to me that respectable people would not allow a little child of nine to run around the streets alone."

My parents discussed the various branches of the Gallard families for a long time, what they'd heard from people close to them or from third parties. Mama got information from the teachers. Andrée's parents were only distantly related to Uncle Jacques's Gallards, but they were very highly regarded. Monsieur Gallard had attended the Polytechnique,* held an excellent post at Citroën, and was the chairman of the League of Fathers of Large Families. His wife, née Rivière de Bonneuil, belonged to a large dynasty of militant Catholics and was well respected by the parishioners of Saint Thomas Aquinas. Informed, most likely, of my mother's concerns, Madame Gallard came to

---

* The École Polytechnique is one of the world's leading universities for science and engineering. [Trans.]

pick up Andrée the following Saturday at the end of the school day. She was a beautiful woman with dark eyes who wore a black velvet ribbon around her neck; it was held in place by an antique pin. She won Mama over by telling her that she looked young enough to be my older sister and by calling her "young lady." But I didn't like her velvet necklace.

Madame Gallard had indulgently told Mama the story of Andrée's martyrdom: the cracked skin, enormous blisters, paraffin-coated dressings, Andrée's delirium, her courage, how one of her little friends had kicked her while they were playing a game and had reopened her wounds. She'd made such an effort not to scream that she'd fainted. When she came to my house to see my notebooks, I looked at her with respect; she took notes in beautiful handwriting, and I thought about her swollen thigh under her pleated skirt. Never had anything as interesting happened to me. I suddenly had the impression that nothing had ever happened to me at all.

All the children I knew bored me, but Andrée made me laugh when we walked together on the playground between classes. She was marvelous at imitating the brusque gestures of Mademoiselle Dubois, the unctuous voice of Mademoiselle Vendroux, the principal. She knew loads of secrets about the place from her older sister: these young women were affiliated with the Jesuits; they wore their hair parted on the side when they were still novices, in the middle once they'd taken their vows. Mademoiselle Dubois, who was only thirty, was the youngest. She'd taken her baccalaureate the year before; the older students had seen her at the Sorbonne, blushing and all awkward in her long skirt. I was a little scandalized by Andrée's irreverence, but I found her funny, and played opposite her when she improvised a dialogue between two of our teachers. Her caricatures were so accurate that we often poked each other with our elbows during lessons when we saw Mademoiselle Dubois open the attendance register or close a book. Once I was so overcome with laughter that I surely would have been thrown out of the class if my behavior hadn't normally been so exemplary.

The first few times I went to play at Andrée's house on the Rue de Grenelle, I was dumbfounded. Apart from her brothers and sisters, there were always masses of cousins and friends; they ran, shouted, sang, dressed up, jumped on the tables, overturned the furniture. Sometimes Malou, who was fifteen and bossy, intervened, but then you'd immediately hear Madame Gallard's voice saying, "Let the children have fun." I was astounded by her indifference to the injuries, bumps, stains, broken dishes. "Mama never gets angry," Andrée said to me with a triumphant smile. At the end of the afternoon, Madame Gallard came into the room we'd wrecked, smiling; she picked up a chair and dried Andrée's forehead, saying, "You're drenched in sweat again!" Andrée hugged her tightly, and for an instant, her face was transformed. I looked away, feeling uneasy, probably because I was a little jealous, perhaps envious, and I felt the kind of fear aroused by the unknown.

I had been taught that I had to love Mama and Papa equally: Andrée didn't hide the fact that she loved her mother more than her father. "Papa is too serious," she calmly said to me one day. Monsieur Gallard puzzled me because he wasn't like Papa. My father never went to Mass, and he smiled whenever someone talked about the miracles of Lourdes in front of him; I'd heard him say that he had only one religion: the love of France. I was not troubled by his irreverence. Mama, who was very pious, seemed to find it normal; a man as superior as Papa necessarily had a more complicated relationship with God than women or little girls did. Monsieur Gallard, on the other hand, took Communion every Sunday with his family; he had a long beard, wore a pince-nez, and volunteered to do good works in his spare time. His silky hair, his Christian virtues, made him seem feminine and belittled him in my eyes. Anyway, he was seen only under unusual circumstances. It was Madame Gallard who ruled the house. I envied the freedom she gave to Andrée, but even though she always spoke to me most kindly, I felt uncomfortable with her.

Sometimes Andrée would say: "I'm tired of playing." We'd go and sit down in Monsieur Gallard's office and not turn on the lights so we wouldn't be discovered, and then we'd chat: it was a new pleasure. My parents talked to me and I talked to them, but we never chatted together; with Andrée, I had real conversations, like Papa did in the evening with Mama. She'd read a lot of books during her long convalescence, and she surprised me because she seemed to believe that the stories the books told had actually happened: she detested Corneille's *Horace* and *Polyeucte*, admired *Don Quixote* and *Cyrano de Bergerac* as if they had existed in flesh and blood. Where earlier centuries were concerned, she also had her favorites. She liked the Greeks, but the Romans bored her; though unmoved by the misfortunes of Louis XVII and his family, she was devastated by the death of Napoleon.

Many of these opinions were subversive, but given her young age, the novices forgave her. "That child has personality," they said at school. Andrée quickly caught up; I only barely beat her in composition, and she had the honor of copying two of her essays into the special book used to display excellent work. She played the piano so well that she was immediately placed in the intermediate group; she also started taking violin lessons. She didn't like to sew, but she was good at it; she competently made caramels, shortbread cookies, chocolate truffles. Even though she was frail, she knew how to turn cartwheels, could do the splits and all sorts of somersaults. But what gave her the greatest prestige in my eyes were certain unique characteristics whose meanings I have never understood: when she looked at a peach or an orchid, or if anyone simply said either word in front of her, Andrée would shudder, and her arms would break out in goose bumps; those were the times when the heavenly gift she'd received—and which I marveled at so much—would manifest itself in the most disconcerting way: it was *character*. I secretly told myself that Andrée was one of those child prodigies whose lives would later be recounted in books.

MOST OF THE PUPILS from the school left Paris in the middle of June because of the bombs and Big Bertha.[*]

The Gallards left for Lourdes; they took part in a large pilgrimage every year. Their son was a stretcher bearer, and the older girls washed dishes in the kitchens of a hospice; I admired the fact that they entrusted Andrée with these grown-up tasks and respected her more for it. Nevertheless, I was proud of the heroic stubbornness of my parents: by remaining in Paris, we were demonstrating to our valiant soldiers that the civilians were "holding out." I was the

---

[*] This was the nickname for the German howitzer cannon. [Trans.]

only one left in my class along with a big idiot who was twelve, and I felt important. One morning when I got to school, the teachers and pupils were all taking refuge in the basement: we joked about that at home for a long time. When the sirens went off, we didn't go down to the basement; the people who lived upstairs came and took shelter at our place, they slept on the couches in the next room. I liked all that hustle and bustle.

I left for Sadernac at the end of July with Mama and my sisters. Grandfather, who remembered the siege of '71, imagined that we were eating rats in Paris: for two months, he stuffed us with chicken and clafoutis cake. I had many happy days. In the living room, there was a library full of old books whose pages were dotted with rust stains; the forbidden works were relegated to the highest shelf, but I was allowed to freely leaf through anything on the lower ones. I read, played with my sisters, and went for long walks. I walked a lot that summer. I walked through the chestnut groves, stinging my fingers; I picked bunches of honeysuckle and spindle, tasted the blackberries, arbutus berries, dogwood leaves, the tart berries of the barberry shrubs; I breathed in the heavy scent of the buckwheat in flower, lay on the ground to catch a whiff of the strange scent of the heather. Then I would sit in the wide meadow, at the foot of the silver poplar trees, and open a novel by James Fenimore Cooper. When the wind blew, the poplars would whisper. The wind enthralled me. I felt that from one end of the earth to the other, the trees spoke to each other and spoke to God; it sounded like both music and a prayer were piercing my heart before rising to the heavens.

The pleasures I experienced were innumerable but difficult to describe. All I sent to Andrée were brief notes on postcards; she hardly wrote to me either. They were in the Landes region, at her maternal grandmother's house; she went horseback riding, she was having a good time; she wouldn't come back to Paris before mid-October. I didn't think of her very often. During the summer vacation, I almost never thought about my life in Paris.

I shed a few tears when saying goodbye to the poplar trees: I was getting older, becoming sentimental. But on the train, I remembered how much I liked the beginning of the school year. Papa was waiting for us on the platform in his pale-blue uniform; he said the war would soon be over. The schoolbooks seemed even newer than in past years: they were bigger, more beautiful, they cracked open beneath your fingers, they smelled good. In the Luxembourg Gardens, there was the stirring scent of dead leaves and dried-out grass. The teachers hugged me effusively, and the homework I'd done over the summer earned me the greatest praise. So why did I feel so miserable? In the evening, after supper, I sat in the adjoining room, reading or writing stories in a notebook; my sisters were asleep; at the end of the hallway, Papa was reading to Mama: it was one of the best moments of the day. I would lie on the red carpet, doing nothing, in a daze. I would look at the enormous wardrobe and the hand-carved wooden clock that held within it two copper pinecones and the obscurity of time. The slats of the heater were set in the wall; through their bronze bars flowed the nauseating smell of warm gusts of air rising from the abyss. All that darkness and the silent things around me suddenly made me feel afraid. I could hear Papa's voice; I knew the title of the book: *Essay on the Inequality of Human Races* by Count de Gobineau. Last year it was *The Origins of Contemporary France* by Taine. Next year, he'll start a new book, and I'll still be here, between the wardrobe and the clock. How many years? How many evenings? Is living nothing more than that: killing one day after the other? Would I be this bored until I died? I thought that I missed Sadernac; before going to bed, I shed a few more tears over the poplar trees.

Two days later, the truth struck me like a lightning bolt. I went into the Sainte Catherine classroom and Andrée smiled at me; I smiled back and we shook hands.

"When did you get back?"

"Last night."

Andrée looked at me somewhat playfully. "You were here the first day of school, of course?"

"Yes," I said. "Did you have a good vacation?" I added.

"Very good, and you?"

"Very good."

We made small talk, like adults do; but I suddenly understood, with astonishment and joy, that the emptiness in my heart, my gloomy feeling of recent days, had only one cause: the absence of Andrée. Living without her was no longer living. Mademoiselle de Villeneuve sat down on her high-backed chair and I thought once more: "Without Andrée, my life is over." My joy transformed into anguish: what would become of me if she died? I wondered. I would be sitting on my little seat, the principal would come in and say in a serious voice: "Let us pray, dear children, your little friend Andrée Gallard was called to God last night." Well! It's simple, I decided, I'd slip under my chair and fall down dead as well. The idea didn't frighten me because we would soon be reunited at the gates of heaven.

On November 11, we celebrated Armistice Day; people hugged and kissed in the street. For four years, I had prayed for this great day to come, and I expected astonishing changes; dark memories returned to my heart. Papa put his civilian clothes back on, but nothing else happened; he talked endlessly about how the Bolsheviks had stolen some of his savings. Those men in some faraway place, whose names dangerously resembled the Boche seemed to possess terrible powers; and then General Foch truly had let himself be manipulated: he might have had to go all the way to Berlin. Papa imagined such a bad future that he didn't dare reopen his office; he found a job at an insurance company and announced it was necessary to tighten our belts. Mama let Elisa go, she didn't behave very well anyway—she went out with firemen every night—and Mama took charge of all the housework; in the evening, she was in a bad mood, Papa too. My sisters often cried. But I didn't care because I had Andrée.

Andrée grew taller and stronger; I stopped thinking she might die, but there was another dangerous threat: the school did not approve of our friendship. Andrée was a brilliant pupil, I came first in the class only because she couldn't be bothered; I admired her nonchalance without being able to imitate it. Nevertheless, she had lost favor with the teachers. They found her contradictory, ironic, prideful; they reproached her for making snide remarks. They never succeeded in catching her being downright insolent because Andrée carefully kept her distance, and that was perhaps what irritated them the most. But they scored a point the day of the piano recital. The great hall was full: in the first rows were the pupils wearing their most beautiful dresses, their hair in ringlets or curls, with bows; behind them, the teachers and supervisors, in silk blouses and white gloves; at the back, the parents and guests. Andrée, dressed in a fancy blue taffeta dress, played a piece that her mother found too difficult for her and in which she normally massacred several bars. I was upset because I could feel all those malevolent eyes fixed on her as she started the tricky passage. She played it without a single mistake, then gave her mother a triumphant look and stuck her tongue out at her. The other mothers coughed, scandalized, the teachers glanced at each other, and the principal turned all red. When Andrée came down from the stage, she ran to her mother, who kissed her. Andrée was laughing in such a happy way that Mademoiselle Vendroux didn't dare scold her. But a few days later, she complained to Mama about Andrée's bad influence on me: we chatted in class, I sniggered, was distracted. She talked about putting us in different classes, and I spent a week in anguish. Madame Gallard, who appreciated my studious enthusiasm, easily convinced Mama to leave us in peace, and as both mothers were excellent patrons with a lot of influence, Mama having three daughters and Madame Gallard six, we continued sitting next to each other as in the past.

Would Andrée have been sad if we'd been prevented from seeing each other? Less than me, most definitely. We were called the inseparable friends, and she liked me more than our other classmates. But it seemed to me that her adoration of her mother made all other feelings fade by comparison. Her family counted a tremendous amount on her; she spent a long time playing with her little twin sisters, bathing and dressing those masses of jumbled flesh. She found meaning in their babbling, their vague gestures, showered them with love. And then there was music, which held an important place in her life. When she sat down at the piano, when she placed her violin in the crook of her neck and listened dreamily to the song born beneath her fingers, I thought I could hear her talking to herself: compared to the long dialogue that continued secretly in her heart, our conversations seemed quite childish. Sometimes Madame Gallard, who played the piano very well, accompanied the piece Andrée was playing on the violin, and then I felt completely excluded. No, our friendship did not have the same importance to Andrée as it did to me, but I admired her far too much to suffer because of it.

The following year, my parents left the apartment on the Boulevard Montparnasse and moved into cramped lodgings on the Rue Cassette, where I didn't have even a corner to myself. Andrée invited me to go and work at her house as often as I wanted. Every time I went into her bedroom, I was so moved that I wanted to make the sign of the Cross. Above her bed was a crucifix with a little branch from a box tree that had been blessed by the priest on Palm Sunday, and opposite, a copy of *Saint Anne* by da Vinci; on the mantelpiece, a portrait of Madame Gallard and a photograph of the château de Béthary. On her bookshelves, Andrée's personal library: *Don Quixote, Gulliver's*

Travels, Eugénie Grandet, Tristan and Isolde (she knew passages from the novel by heart); she usually liked realist or satirical books: her preference for that romantic epic confused me. I anxiously examined the walls and objects that surrounded Andrée. I wanted to understand what she was thinking when her bow glided over the strings of her violin. I wanted to know why, with so much emotion in her heart, so many things to do, so many gifts, she often looked distant and seemed sad to me. She was very pious. When I went to pray in the chapel, I sometimes found her kneeling at the foot of the altar, head in her hands, or her arms outstretched in front of one of the stations of the Cross. Was she considering becoming a nun later in life? Yet her freedom and the joys of the world were so important to her. Her eyes shone when she told me about her vacation: she spent hours galloping on horseback through the pine forests where the low branches scratched her face, she swam in the stagnant waters of the ponds, in the brisk waters of the Adour River. Was that the paradise she was dreaming of when she sat motionless in front of her notebooks, staring into space? One day, she noticed I was watching her and laughed, embarrassed: "You think I'm wasting my time?"

"Me? Not at all!"

Andrée stared at me somewhat mockingly. "Don't you ever dream about things? Doesn't that ever happen to you?"

"No," I replied humbly.

What would I have dreamed about? I loved Andrée more than anything, and she was here with me.

I didn't dream, I always learned my lessons, I was interested in everything. Andrée made fun of me a little; she made fun of just about everyone. I happily took her teasing. Once, however, she hurt me badly. That year, unusually, I spent the Easter vacation in Sadernac. I discovered springtime and was ecstatic. I sat down at one of the garden tables with some blank sheets of paper and for two hours described to Andrée the new grass dotted with cowslips and primroses, the scent of the wisteria, the blue sky, and the great emotion in my soul. She did not reply. When I first saw her again in the school's coatroom, I asked her about it.

"Why didn't you write to me?" I said reproachfully. "Didn't you get my letter?"

"I got it," said Andrée.

"Well then, you're damned lazy!" I said.

Andrée began to laugh. "I thought you'd accidentally sent me the homework about your vacation . . ."

I could feel myself blushing. "Homework?"

"Come on, you didn't churn out all that prose just for me!" said Andrée. "I'm sure it was a study for a composition: 'Describe the springtime.'"

"No," I said. "It was probably bad prose, but I did write that letter just for you."

The young Boulard children were coming over to us, curious and talkative, so we left it at that. But in class, I messed up my Latin analysis. Andrée had found my letter ridiculous, which hurt me; but more importantly, she had no idea how much I needed to share everything with her. That was what saddened me the most: I had just realized that she had absolutely no idea of my feelings for her.

We left school together; Mama didn't take me anymore, and I normally went home with Andrée. Suddenly, she linked elbows with me: it was a surprising gesture, we always kept our distance.

"Sylvie, I'm sorry about what I said to you before," she said quickly, "it was pure spitefulness: I know very well that your letter wasn't vacation homework."

"I suppose it was ridiculous," I said.

"Not at all! The truth is, I was in a foul mood the day I got it, and you sounded so joyful!"

"Why were you in such a bad mood?" I asked.

Andrée stood silent for a moment.

"Just like that, no reason; just everything." She hesitated. "I'm tired of being a child," she suddenly said. "Don't you find it endless?"

I looked at her in astonishment. Andrée had much more freedom than I did; and even though things weren't much fun at home, I had no desire to get older. The idea that I was already thirteen frightened me.

"No," I said. "The life that adults lead seems so monotonous to me; all their days are the same, they stop learning things . . ."

"Oh! Studying isn't all that counts in life," said Andrée, sounding impatient.

I would have liked to protest: "There isn't just studying, there's you." But we had changed the conversation. In books, I thought with sadness, people declare their love or hatred for each other, they dare admit to everything they feel in their hearts; why is that impossible in life? I would walk for two days and two nights without eating or drinking to see Andrée for an hour, to spare her any pain: and she had no idea!

For several days, I sadly hashed over those thoughts, then had a revelation: I'd make Andrée a gift for her birthday.

Parents are unpredictable; normally, Mama found my ideas absurd a priori, but the idea of the gift was approved. I decided to use a pattern from *La mode pratique* to make a handbag that would be the height of luxury. I chose some red and blue silk and gold brocade, thick and lustrous, that looked as beautiful as a fairy tale. I mounted it on a wicker frame that I made myself. I hated sewing, but I worked so hard that once it was finished, the bag was really beautiful; it had a cherry-colored silk lining and a patch pocket. I wrapped it in tissue paper, put it in a box, and tied it with a ribbon. The day of Andrée's thirteenth birthday, Mama came with me to her party; people were already there, and I felt intimidated as I handed the box to Andrée:

"This is for your birthday," I said.

She looked at me with surprise.

"I made it myself," I added.

She unwrapped the sparkling handbag and her cheeks turned slightly red. "Sylvie! This is amazing! You're so kind!"

I thought that if our mothers hadn't been there, she would have kissed me.

"Thank Madame Lepage as well," said Madame Gallard in a friendly voice. "Because she was undoubtedly the one who did all the work . . ."

"Thank you, Madame," Andrée said quickly. Then she smiled at me, in a way that showed she was touched. While Mama was protesting somewhat, I felt a little knot forming in my stomach. I had just realized that Madame Gallard didn't like me anymore.

TODAY, I admire the insight of that vigilant woman: the fact is, I was changing. I was beginning to find our teachers total fools; I enjoyed asking them embarrassing questions, stood up to them, met their observations with impertinence. Mama scolded me a little, but when I told Papa about my quarrels with the teachers, he laughed; and that laugh removed any scruples I might have had. Besides, I couldn't imagine for an instant that God would be offended by my misconduct. When I went to confession, I didn't bother with childish things. I took Communion several times a week, and Father Dominique encouraged me to follow the path of spiritual contemplation: my secular life had nothing to do with that holy venture. The sins I accused myself of concerned my conscience: I'd lacked enthusiasm, forgotten about the presence of God for too long, was distracted when I prayed, thought about myself with too much indulgence. I had just reached the end of explaining these faults when I heard Father Dominique's voice through the peephole: "Is that everything?"

I sat dumbstruck.

"I've been told that my little Sylvie is no longer the same as in the past," said the voice. "It seems she has become distracted, disobedient, insolent."

My cheeks turned bright red and I couldn't manage to get out a single word.

"From now on, you must beware of those things," said the voice. "We'll talk about it together."

Father Dominique absolved me, and I left the confessional, my face on fire; I ran out of the chapel without doing my penance. I was far more shaken up than the day when a man in the Métro had opened his raincoat to show me something pink.

For eight years, I had knelt before Father Dominique the way you kneel before God: and he was nothing more than an old blabbermouth who prattled with the teachers and took their gossip seriously. I was ashamed to have opened up my soul to him: he had betrayed me. From that point on, whenever I saw him in the corridor in his black robes, I would blush and run away.

During the end of that year and for the following year, I went to confession with the vicars at the Église Saint Sulpice; I changed where I went often. I continued to pray and meditate, but during the summer vacation, I had a revelation. I still loved Sadernac, and went for many long walks, as in the past; but now the blackberries and hazelnuts in the hedges bored me, I wanted to taste the milk of the euphorbias, bite into the poisonous berries the color of rust that bear the beautiful, enigmatic name "Solomon's seal." I did a great deal of forbidden things: I ate apples in between meals, secretly took novels by Alexandre Dumas off the top shelf in the library. I had illuminating conversations with the tenant farmer's daughter about the mystery of birth; at night, in my bed, I told myself bizarre stories that put me in strange moods. One evening, lying in a damp meadow, looking up at the moon, I thought: "I'm sinning!" but I was resolutely determined to continue to eat, read, speak, and dream in whatever way I pleased. "I don't believe in God!" I thought. How was it possible to believe in God and deliberately choose to disobey Him? I sat stunned for a moment by this revelation: I did not believe.

Neither Papa nor the writers I admired were believers; and while the world probably could not be explained without God, God really didn't explain that much, and besides, no one understood anything about Him. I easily adjusted to my new frame of mind. Nevertheless, when I got back to Paris, I was overcome with panic. You can't help thinking what you think: but still, in the past, Papa talked about shooting the defeatists, and the year before, one of the older pupils had been expelled from school because, or so it was whispered, she had lost her faith. I would have to carefully hide my fall from grace; at night, I would wake up in a sweat at the idea that Andrée might suspect.

Fortunately, we never talked about either sexuality or religion. Many other problems had begun to preoccupy us. We were studying the French Revolution; we admired Camille Desmoulins,* Madame Roland,† and even Dan-

---

* Camille Desmoulins (1760–1794) was a journalist and politician who was executed along with Danton. [Trans.]

† Marie-Jeanne Roland (1754–1793) was a writer who held a literary "salon" and became involved in politics. She was executed for treason and, as she climbed the steps of the guillotine, said, "O Liberty, what crimes are committed in thy name." [Trans.]

ton. We endlessly discussed justice, equality, propriety. On such matters, the opinions of the teachers counted for nothing, while our parents had old-fashioned ideas that we no longer agreed with. My father happily read *L'action française.** Monsieur Gallard was more democratic; he had been interested in Marc Sangnier† in his youth. But he was no longer young and explained to Andrée that any form of socialism necessarily brings with it a dumbing down and the abolition of spiritual values. He didn't convince us, but some of his arguments worried us. We tried to have discussions with Malou's friends, older girls who would have known much more than we did; but they thought like Monsieur Gallard, and such questions didn't interest them much. They preferred talking about music, painting, and literature, in a rather stupid way, actually.

When Malou was entertaining, she often asked us to come and serve the tea, but she felt we had little respect for her guests, so she tried to get back at Andrée by acting superior. One afternoon, Isabelle Barrière, who, very conveniently, was in love with her piano teacher—a married man with three children—brought the conversation around to romantic novels. Malou, her cousin Guite, and

---

* A Royalist, nationalistic newspaper founded in 1908 and censored after the Liberation in 1944. [Trans.]

† Marc Sangnier (1873–1950) was a Roman Catholic thinker and politician. [Trans.]

the Gosselin sisters took turns saying which ones they preferred.

"What about you, Andrée?" Isabelle asked.

"Romantic novels bore me," Andrée said, quite definitively.

"Really!" said Malou. "Everyone knows that you know *Tristan and Isolde* by heart."

Malou added that she didn't like that story; Isabelle did like it; she declared dreamily that she found that epic of platonic love very moving. Andrée burst out laughing.

"Platonic, the love between Tristan and Isolde! No," she said, "there's nothing platonic about it."

There was an embarrassed silence.

"Little girls shouldn't talk about things they know nothing about," said Guite, curtly.

Andrée laughed again without replying. I stared at her, confused. What exactly did she mean? I had only one idea of love: the love I felt for her.

"Poor Isabelle!" Andrée said once we were back in her room. "She's going to have to forget her Tristan: she's almost engaged to an awful bald man," she sneered. "I hope she believes in love at first sacrament."

"What's that?"

"My aunt Louise, Guite's mother, claims that the moment the engaged couple says 'I do,' they fall madly in love with each other. You can see how useful that theory is to mothers; no need to think about their daughters' feelings: God will provide."

"No one can believe that's true, surely," I said.

"Guite does." Andrée fell silent, then continued: "Mama doesn't go that far, of course, but she does say that once you're married, you're blessed."

She glanced over at the picture of her mother.

"Mama was very happy with Papa," she said hesitantly, "yet if Grandmother hadn't forced her, she wouldn't have married him. She turned him down twice."

I looked at the photo of Madame Gallard: it was strange to think she'd once had the heart of a young girl.

"She turned him down!"

"Yes. Papa seemed too austere to her. But he loved her and wouldn't be discouraged. She started to love him too after they got engaged," Andrée added without much conviction.

We thought for a moment in silence.

"It can't be much fun living day in, day out, with someone you don't love," I said.

"That must be horrible," said Andrée. She shuddered, as if she had seen an orchid; her arms broke out in goose bumps. "They teach us in catechism class that we have to respect our bodies: so selling yourself in marriage is just as bad as selling yourself outside of marriage," she said.

"No one is forced to get married," I said.

"I'll get married," said Andrée, "but not before I'm twenty-two." She suddenly put our collection of Latin texts on the table. "Shall we get to work?"

I sat down next to her and we concentrated on the translation of the Battle of Lake Trasimene.

We no longer served tea to Malou's friends. Decidedly, to answer the questions that preoccupied us, we had to count only on ourselves. Never had we talked as much as that year. And despite the secret that I did not share with her, never had we been as close as then. We were allowed to go to the Odéon movie theater to see all the great classics. We discovered the literature of the Romantic era: I raved about Hugo, Andrée preferred Musset, we both admired Vigny. We started planning for the future. It was agreed that after my baccalaureate, I would continue my studies; Andrée hoped she would be allowed to take courses at the Sorbonne. At the end of the trimester, I had the greatest joy of my childhood: Madame Gallard unexpectedly invited me to spend two weeks in Béthary, and Mama agreed.

I expected Andrée to be waiting for me at the station, but when I got off the train, I was surprised to find Madame Gallard. She was wearing a black-and-white dress, a large black straw hat decorated with daisies, and a white silk ribbon around her neck. She moved her lips toward my forehead without actually kissing me.

"Did you have a good trip, my little Sylvie?"

"Very good, Madame," then I added, "but I'm afraid I'm all covered in coal dust."

In Madame Gallard's presence, I always felt vaguely guilty. My hands were dirty, my face as well, most likely; but she seemed not to care, she seemed distracted. She smiled at the employee out of habit, then headed toward an English-style carriage with a bay horse. She untied the reins from the stake and quickly climbed in.

"Come along."

I sat down next to her; she held the reins loosely in her gloved hands.

"I wanted to speak to you before you see Andrée," she said, without looking at me.

I stiffened. What advice was she going to give me? Had she guessed that I was no longer a believer? But then why did she invite me?

"Andrée is upset, and you have to help me."

"Andrée is upset?" I repeated, like an idiot.

I was embarrassed that Madame Gallard was suddenly talking to me as she would to an adult, there was something suspicious about it. She tugged on the reins and clicked her tongue; the horse started to move, slowly.

"Has Andrée ever spoken to you about her friend Bernard?"

"No."

The carriage followed a dusty road, lined with locust trees. Madame Gallard sat silent.

"Bernard's father owns the estate next to my mother's," she finally said. "He comes from one of the Basque families who made their fortune in Argentina: that's where his father lives most of the time, along with his wife and other children. But Bernard was a frail child, he couldn't take the climate there: he spent his entire childhood here, with an elderly aunt and private tutors."

Madame Gallard turned toward me.

"You know that after her accident, Andrée stayed at Béthary for a year, lying on her back on a stiff board; Bernard came to play with her every day. She was alone, in pain, bored, and, of course, given their age at the time, it didn't matter," she said in a remorseful tone of voice, which confused me.

"Andrée didn't tell me about that," I said.

I felt a lump in my throat. I wanted to jump out of the carriage and flee, like the day I had rushed out of the confessional, away from Father Dominique.

"They saw each other every summer, went riding together. They were still only children. Only they've grown up."

Madame Gallard looked straight at me; there was something in her eyes, something like pleading.

"You see, Sylvie, it is absolutely out of the question that Bernard and Andrée ever marry; Bernard's father is just as opposed to the idea as we are. So I have forbidden Andrée from seeing him again."

"I understand," I ventured, stammering.

"She's taken it very badly," said Madame Gallard. Once again, she shot me a look that was both suspicious and imploring. "I'm counting on you a lot."

"But what can I do?" I asked.

The words came out of my mouth but made no sense, and I didn't understand the sounds reaching my ears; my head was full of noise and darkness.

"Distract her, talk to her about things that interest her. And then, if you have the opportunity, try to reason with her. I'm afraid she will fall ill. Right now, *I* can't say anything to her," Madame Gallard added.

She was clearly worried and unhappy, but I wasn't moved by her: quite the opposite, at that moment, I hated her.

"I'll try," I murmured, grudgingly.

The horse trotted along the avenue lined with white oak trees and stopped in front of a large manor house with walls covered in Virginia creeper: I'd seen a photograph of it on Andrée's mantelpiece. I now knew why she loved Béthary and the horseback riding she did there; I understood what she was thinking about when she stared out into space.

"Hello!"

Andrée walked down the front steps, smiling; she was wearing a white dress with a green necklace, her short hair was as shiny as a helmet. She looked like a real young lady, and I suddenly thought that she was very pretty: it was an incongruous idea; we hardly attached any importance to beauty.

"I think that Sylvie wants to freshen up; and then you can come down to dinner," said Madame Gallard.

I followed Andrée through the entrance hall that smelled of crème caramel, fresh wax, and an old granary. Doves cooed; someone was playing the piano. We went upstairs and Andrée opened a door.

"Mama's put you in my room," she said.

There was a large canopy bed with spiral columns and, at the other end of the room, a narrow divan. How happy I would have been an hour earlier at the idea of sharing Andrée's room! But now I went inside with a heavy heart. Madame Gallard was using me: so she would be forgiven? To distract Andrée? To keep an eye on her? What exactly was she afraid of?

Andrée walked over to the window.

"When there's clear weather," she said listlessly, "you can see the Pyrenees."

Night fell, there was no clear weather. I washed and

fixed my hair, and talked about my journey without much enthusiasm. I'd taken the train alone for the first time; it had been an adventure, but I found nothing more to say about it.

"You should cut your hair," said Andrée.

"Mama doesn't want me to," I said.

Mama thought that short hair made you look disreputable, so I pinned my hair back in a boring bun.

"Let's go downstairs," said Andrée. "I'll show you the library."

Someone was still playing the piano and children were singing; the house was full of sound: dishes rattling, footsteps. I went into the library: the complete collection of *Revue des deux mondes*,* from the very first issue, the works of Louis Veuillot† and Montalembert,‡ the sermons of Lacordaire,§ the speeches of the Count de Mun,¶ everything by Joseph

---

* A monthly magazine with literary, political, and cultural articles, first published in 1829. [Trans.]

† Louis Veuillot (1813–1883) was a journalist and author who helped to popularize "ultramontanism," a philosophy that favored papal supremacy. [Trans.]

‡ Charles de Montalembert (1810–1870) was a prominent supporter of liberal Catholicism. [Trans.]

§ Jean-Baptiste Lacordaire (1802–1861) was a theologian and political activist who re-established the Dominican Order after the French Revolution. [Trans.]

¶ Albert, Count de Mun (1841–1914), was a Christian Socialist leader

de Maistre.* On the pedestal tables were photographs of men with sideburns and old men with beards; Andrée's ancestors: they had all been militant Catholics.

Even though they were dead, you could feel they were at home here, and amid all those austere gentlemen, Andrée seemed out of place: too young, too delicate, and, especially, too alive.

A bell rang and we went through to the dining room. There were so many of them! I knew everyone except the grandmother: she had white hair that she wore coiled around her head and the classic face of a grandmother; that was my only impression of her. Andrée's older brother was wearing a soutane; he had just entered the seminary. He was having a discussion with Malou and Monsieur Gallard about women's suffrage, which seemed to be a regular topic. Yes, it was scandalous that the mother of a family had fewer rights than a drunken laborer, but Monsieur Gallard objected that in the working classes, there were more women Communists than men; when all was said and done, if the law passed, it would serve the enemies of the Church. Andrée kept silent. At the end of the table,

---

who advocated Roman Catholicism as an instrument of social reform. [Trans.]

* Joseph de Maistre (1753–1821) was a philosopher and moralist who advocated conservatism. [Trans.]

the twin girls were throwing bits of bread at each other; Madame Gallard smiled and did nothing. For the first time, I clearly realized that her smile hid a trap. I had often envied Andrée's independence; suddenly, she seemed a lot less free than I was. Behind her, she had this past; around her, this large house, this enormous family: a prison whose exits were carefully guarded.

"Well? What do you think of us?" said Malou, getting straight to the point.

"Me? Nothing, why?"

"You've been looking all around the table: you were thinking something."

"That there were so many of you, that's all," I said.

I told myself that I had to learn how to keep my face from giving me away.

"You should show Sylvie the grounds," Madame Gallard said to Andrée as we got up from the table.

"Yes," said Andrée.

"Take your coats, it's cool out at night."

Andrée took down two loden wool coats hanging in the hallway. The doves were asleep. We went out the back door that led to the servants' quarters. Between the storeroom and the woodshed, a wolfdog was whimpering as she pulled at her chain. Andrée went over to the doghouse. "Come on, my poor little Mirza," she said, "I'll take you for a walk, poor thing."

She untied the animal, who leaped joyously on her, then ran off ahead of us.

"Do you think that animals have a soul?" Andrée asked.

"I don't know."

"If they don't, that's just too unfair! They're just as unhappy as people are. And they don't understand why," Andrée added. "It's worse when you don't understand."

I didn't reply. I had waited for this evening for so long! I'd told myself that I would at last be taken into the heart of Andrée's life; yet never had she seemed so distant: she was no longer the same Andrée since her secret had a name. We walked silently down poorly kept paths where mallow and cornflowers grew. The grounds were full of beautiful trees and flowers.

"Let's sit down over there," said Andrée, pointing to a bench at the foot of a cedar. She took out a pack of Gauloise cigarettes. "Do you want one?"

"No," I said. "Since when do you smoke?"

"Mama forbids it; but when you start to disobey . . ."

She lit a cigarette, sending smoke rising into her eyes. I gathered my courage:

"Andrée, what's going on? Tell me."

"I suppose that Mama put you in the picture," said Andrée. "She insisted on going to pick you up . . ."

"She told me about your friend Bernard. You never told me anything about him."

"I couldn't talk about Bernard," said Andrée. Her left hand opened and closed in a kind of spasm. "Now it's public knowledge."

"We don't have to talk about it if you don't want to," I said quickly.

"With you, it's different," Andrée said, looking at me. "With you, I do want to talk about it." She diligently inhaled a bit of smoke. "What did Mama tell you?"

"How you and Bernard became friends and that she's forbidden you from ever seeing him again."

"She's forbidden me," said Andrée, throwing the cigarette on the ground and crushing it with the heel of her shoe. "The night I arrived, I went for a walk with Bernard, after dinner; I got back late. Mama was waiting for me, and I could tell right away that she had a strange look on her face; she asked me a lot of questions."

Andrée shrugged. "She asked me if we had kissed!" she said, sounding annoyed. "Of course we kissed! We love each other."

I lowered my head. Andrée was unhappy and I couldn't bear that idea; but her unhappiness was strange to me. The kind of love that involved kissing had no reality for me.

"Mama said horrible things to me," Andrée said, wrapping her coat tighter around her.

"But why?"

"His parents are a lot richer than we are, but they're not part of our social circle, not at all. It seems that over there, in Rio, they lead an odd kind of life, very undisciplined," said Andrée, sounding puritanical. "And Bernard's mother is Jewish," she added quietly.

I looked at Mirza, motionless on the grass, her ears pointing to the stars: I was as incapable of translating what I felt into words as she was.

"And?" I asked.

"Mama went and spoke to Bernard's father; he agreed completely: I wasn't a good match. He decided to take Bernard to Biarritz for the summer vacation, then they'll head back to Argentina. Bernard is quite healthy now."

"Has he already left?"

"Yes; Mama forbade me from saying goodbye to him, but I disobeyed her," said Andrée. "You can't know how awful it is to make someone you love suffer." Her voice was trembling. "He cried; how he cried!"

"How old is he?" I asked. "What's he like?"

"He's fifteen, like me. But he knows nothing about life," said Andrée. "No one ever cared about him, I was the only one he had. I have a small photograph of him," she said, searching through her handbag.

I looked at the young boy I didn't know who loved Andrée, whom she had kissed, and who had cried so much.

He had large, pale, bulging eyes and dark hair cut in the style of the Roman emperor Caracalla; he looked like Saint Tarcisius, the Christian martyr.

"He has the eyes and cheeks of a real little boy," said Andrée, "but you can see how sad his mouth is: he seems to be apologizing for being on this earth."

She leaned her head against the back of the bench and looked up at the sky. "Sometimes I tell myself that I'd prefer him to be dead; at least I'd be the only one suffering."

Andrée's hand convulsed again. "I can't stand the idea that at this very moment, he's crying."

"You will see each other again!" I said. "You'll see each other again because you love each other! One day you'll be adults."

"In six years: that's too long. At our age, that's too long. No," said Andrée in despair, "I know very well that I'll never see him again."

Never! It was the first time that word struck my heart with all its weight; beneath the endless sky, I repeated it to myself, and wanted to cry out.

"When I got home after having said goodbye to him forever," said Andrée, "I climbed up onto the roof of the house: I wanted to jump."

"You wanted to kill yourself?"

"I stayed there for two hours; it took two hours to

make up my mind. I told myself it didn't matter if I were damned: if God is not good, I don't want to go to His heaven."

Andrée shrugged. "But I was still afraid. Oh! Not of dying, quite the opposite, I so longed to be dead! But fear of hell. If I go to hell, it's for eternity; I would never see Bernard again."

"You will see him again in this world!" I said.

"It's over," Andrée said, shaking her head.

She suddenly stood up.

"Let's go back. I'm cold."

We walked across the lawn in silence. Andrée tied Mirza up and we went upstairs to our bedroom. I slept in the canopy bed and she slept on the foldout sofa. She turned off the light.

"I didn't admit to Mama that I'd seen Bernard again," she said. "I don't want to hear the things she'd say to me."

I hesitated. I didn't like Madame Gallard, but I owed Andrée the truth.

"She's very worried about you," I said.

"Yes, I suppose she's concerned," said Andrée.

ANDRÉE DIDN'T mention Bernard during the days that followed, and I didn't dare be the first to bring him up. In the morning, she played her violin for a long time, and almost always sad pieces. Then we'd go out into the sunshine. This part of the country was dryer than where I'm from; along its dusty roads, I discovered the acrid scent of the fig trees. In the forest, I tasted the pine nuts, licked the drops of resin that had solidified on the pine trees. When we got back from our walk, Andrée would go into the stable and stroke her little chestnut horse, but she never rode him again.

Our afternoons were not as calm. Madame Gallard had decided to see Malou married, so to camouflage the visits of boys who were more or less strangers, she opened up the house to all the "respectable" young people in the area. We played croquet or tennis or danced on the lawns, made small talk while eating cakes. The day that Malou came out of her room in an ecru silk shantung dress, her hair freshly washed and curled with a little curling iron, Andrée poked me with her elbow.

"She's dressed up to meet someone."

Malou spent the afternoon with a very ugly man from the Saint Cyr military academy who didn't play tennis, didn't dance, didn't speak: every now and again, he would pick up our tennis balls. After he left, Madame Gallard locked herself in the library with her oldest daughter; the window was open, so we could hear Malou's voice: "No, Mama, not him: he's too boring!"

"Poor Malou!" said Andrée. "All the guys she meets are so stupid and so ugly!"

She sat down on the swing and took hold of its ropes. Next to the shed, there was a kind of open-air gymnasium. Andrée often practiced on the trapezium or the horizontal bar; she was very good at it.

"Push me," she said.

I pushed; when she'd picked up some speed, she stood up and gave a mighty kick: soon the swing was flying toward the tops of the trees.

"Not so high!" I shouted.

She didn't reply; she flew upward, swooped down, soared even higher. The twin girls, who were playing with the sawdust from the logs next to the dog's kennel, had looked up, interested. You could hear the dull thud of tennis balls being hit in the distance. Andrée was skimming the leaves of the maple trees, and I was starting to get frightened: I could hear the steel hooks on the swing creaking.

"Andrée!"

The entire house was peaceful; through the basement window, muffled sounds rose from the kitchen; the larkspur and money plant that lined the wall barely moved. But I was afraid. I didn't dare grab on to the seat of the swing or plead too much; I thought the swing was going to turn upside down, or that Andrée would be overcome by dizziness and would let go of the ropes. Just watching her flying up and down in the sky like a pendulum gone mad made me feel nauseated. Why was she swinging for such a long time? When she flew close to me, straight and tall in her white dress, her eyes stared blankly ahead, and her lips were tightly shut. Perhaps something in her mind had cracked and she could no longer stop. The dinner bell rang, and Mirza started to howl. Andrée continued flying through the trees. "She's going to kill herself," I thought.

"Andrée!"

Someone else had shouted. Madame Gallard came over to us, her face furious. "Come down at once! That is an order. Come down!"

Andrée blinked and looked down at the ground; she bent her knees, sat down, and used her feet to brake so forcefully that she was flung forward onto the lawn.

"Did you hurt yourself?"

"No."

She started laughing; her laughter ended in a hiccup and she stayed glued to the ground, eyes closed.

"Of course you've made yourself sick!" said Madame Gallard harshly. "Half an hour on that swing! How old are you?"

Andrée opened her eyes. "The sky is spinning."

"You were supposed to make a fruit cake for tomorrow's tea party."

"I'll do it after dinner," said Andrée, standing up. She put her hand on my shoulder. "I'm reeling."

Madame Gallard walked away; she took the twins by the hand and led them back to the house. Andrée looked up at the tops of the trees.

"I feel good up there," she said.

"You frightened me," I said.

"Oh! The swing is sturdy, there's never been an accident," said Andrée.

No, she hadn't thought of killing herself, that was settled; but when I recalled her staring eyes and tightly closed lips, I was afraid.

After dinner, when the kitchen was empty, Andrée headed downstairs and I went with her; it was an enormous room that took up half the basement. During the day, you could see things passing by its little window: legs, guinea fowl, dogs, human feet. But at this time of day, nothing moved outside, only Mirza on her chain whimpered softly. The embers were purring in the cast-iron stove; no other sound was heard. While Andrée cracked the eggs and added the sugar and yeast, I surveyed the walls, opened the sideboards. The copper pans sparkled: rows of saucepans, cauldrons, skimming ladles, basins, bed warmers that, in the past, had warmed the sheets of her bearded ancestors; on the dresser, I admired the set of enameled plates in simple colors. Made of cast iron, earthenware, stoneware, porcelain, aluminum, tin—countless covered pots, frying pans, casseroles, stewpots, oven dishes, porringers, soup tureens, platters, metal tumblers, strainers, meat cleavers, mills, molds, and mortars! What a variety of bowls, cups, glasses, champagne flutes and coupes, plates, saucers, gravy boats, jars, jugs, pitchers, carafes! Did every type of spoon, ladle, fork, and knife truly have a particular use? Did we really have so many different needs to satisfy? This secret world should have been revealed above ground through enormous, sophisticated celebrations which, to my knowledge, were unique to this place.

"Is everything used?" I asked Andrée.

"More or less: there are heaps of rituals," she said. She put the pale cake batter in the oven. "You haven't seen anything," she said. "Come and have a tour of the cellar."

We first crossed through the dairy: glazed earthenware jars and bowls, polished wooden churns, blocks of butter, shimmering *fromage blanc* cheese covered with white muslin: this sterility and the smell of babies made me want to flee. I preferred the wine cellars packed with dusty bottles and little casks full of liquor; but the abundance of hams, dried sausages, piles of onions and potatoes overwhelmed me.

"This is why she needs to fly up into the trees," I thought, looking at Andrée.

"Do you like cherries in brandy?"

"I've never tried them."

There were hundreds of pots of jam on the shelves: each one had a parchment label with a date and the name of the fruit. There were also jars of fruit preserves conserved in syrup and liquor. Andrée took one of the jars of cherries and carried it into the kitchen. She put it down on the table. Using a wooden ladle, she filled two bowls; she tasted the pink liquid right from the ladle.

"Grandmother was heavy-handed," she said. "You'd get drunk pretty easily on this!"

I grabbed the stem of a faded piece of fruit. It was a little wilted, wrinkly: it no longer tasted like a cherry, but I liked the warmth of the liquor.

"Have you ever gotten drunk?" I asked.

Andrée's face lit up.

"Once, with Bernard. We drank a small bottle of Chartreuse. At first, it was funny: everything was spinning around even more than when I got off the swing; but afterward, we felt nauseated."

The stove hummed; we could just smell the slight scent of baking. Since Andrée had mentioned Bernard herself, I dared to question her.

"Was it after your accident that you became friends? Did he come to see you often?"

"Yes. We played checkers, cards, and dominoes. Bernard could have bad tantrums back then; once, I accused him of cheating, and he kicked me straight in my right thigh; he didn't do it on purpose. I fainted from the pain. By the time I came to, he'd called for help and they were changing my bandages; and he was sobbing at the foot of my bed."

Andrée stared out into the distance.

"Never had I seen a little boy cry; my brother and cousins were brutes. Once they'd left us alone, we kissed . . ."

Andrée filled our bowls again; the smell was getting stronger; we could tell that the cake in the oven was turning golden brown. Mirza wasn't whimpering anymore, she must have been asleep, everyone was asleep.

"He started loving me," said Andrée. She turned to look at me. "I can't explain it to you: that made such a change in my life! I had always thought that no one could love me."

I flinched. "You thought that?"

"Yes."

"But why?" I said, outraged.

"I thought I was so ugly, so awkward, so uninteresting," she said, shrugging. "And it was also true that no one cared about me."

"What about your mother?"

"Oh! A mother has to love her children, that doesn't count. Mama loved all of us, and there were so many of us!"

There was disgust in her voice. Had she been jealous of

her brothers and sisters? Had she suffered from the coldness that I could feel in Madame Gallard? It had never occurred to me that her love for her mother might have been an unhappy kind of love. She pressed her hands against the gleaming wooden table.

"Bernard was the only one in the world who loved me for myself, just as I was, and because I was who I am," she said passionately.

"What about me?" I asked.

The words had just slipped out: I felt outraged at so much injustice. Andrée stared at me in surprise.

"You?"

"Didn't I care about you for who you are?"

"Of course," said Andrée, sounding vague.

The warmth of the liquor and my indignation made me bolder; I wanted to say things to Andrée that are said only in books.

"You never knew this, but from the day I met you, you've meant everything to me," I said. "I'd decided that if you died, I would die immediately."

I was speaking of the past, and tried to sound detached. Andrée continued looking at me, confused. "I thought it was only your books and studies that truly counted for you."

"You came first," I said. "I would have given up everything not to lose you."

She kept silent.

"You didn't know?" I asked.

"When you gave me that handbag for my birthday, I thought that you really cared about me."

"It was a lot more than that!" I said sadly.

She seemed touched. Why hadn't I known how to make her sense my love? I had believed she was so admired that I thought she was fulfilled, happy. I felt like crying over her, and over me.

"It's funny," said Andrée, "we've been inseparable for so many years, and I now realize that I don't know you well at all! I judge people too quickly," she said, sounding remorseful.

I didn't want her to blame herself.

"I didn't know you that well either," I said with feeling. "I thought you were proud to be the way you are; I envied you."

"I'm not proud," she said.

She stood up and walked over to the stove.

"The cake's ready," she said, opening the oven door.

She turned off the oven and put the cake in the pantry. We went up to our bedroom.

"Will you take Communion tomorrow?" she asked while we were getting undressed.

"No," I said.

"Then we'll go to High Mass together tomorrow. I'm

not taking Communion either. I'm in a state of sin," she added coolly. "I still haven't told Mama that I disobeyed her, and the worst part is that I'm not sorry."

I slipped under my sheets, between the twisted columns. "You couldn't have let Bernard leave without seeing him again."

"I couldn't!" said Andrée. "He would have thought I was indifferent; he would have been even more devastated. I couldn't," she said again.

"Then you were right to disobey," I said.

"Oh!" said Andrée. "Sometimes, no matter what you do, everything is bad."

She got into bed but left the blue light on her night table on.

"It's one of those things I don't understand," she said. "Why doesn't God tell us clearly what He wants of us?"

I didn't reply; Andrée shifted in her bed, rearranged the pillows.

"I want to ask you something."

"Go ahead."

"Do you still believe in God?"

I didn't hesitate; tonight, the truth did not frighten me.

"I don't believe anymore," I said. "I haven't believed in a year."

"I thought so," said Andrée.

She propped herself up against her pillows.

"Sylvie! It isn't possible that there is only this life!"

"I don't believe anymore," I said again.

"Sometimes it's difficult," said Andrée. "Why does God want us to be unhappy? My brother tells me that's the problem of evil, that the priests in the Church resolved it a long time ago. He repeats what he was taught in the seminary, but I'm not convinced."

"No," I said, "if God exists, evil is not comprehensible."

"But maybe we have to accept that we can't understand," said Andrée. "It's prideful to want to understand everything."

She switched off the night-light.

"There's surely an afterlife," she added softly. "There has to be an afterlife!"

I don't know exactly what I expected when I woke up, but I was disappointed. Andrée was just the same, so was I, and we said good morning as we always had. My disappointment continued over the following days. Of course, we were so close that it was impossible to get any closer; saying a few things doesn't carry much weight after six years of friendship. But when I thought back to that hour spent in the kitchen, I was sad to think that, in truth, nothing had happened.

One morning, we were sitting under a fig tree, eating figs; the fat purple figs sold in Paris have no taste at all, but I loved this pale fruit, bursting with grainy jam.

"I talked to Mama last night," Andrée told me.

I felt a twinge in my heart; Andrée seemed closer to me when she was distant from her mother.

"She asked me if I'd take Communion on Sunday. It upset her a lot that I didn't last Sunday."

"Did she guess why?"

"Not exactly. But I told her."

"Ah! You told her?"

Andrée pressed her cheek against the fig tree.

"Poor Mama! She's so worried about everything now: because of Malou and now because of me!"

"Did she get mad at you?"

"She said that as far as she was concerned, she forgave me, and the rest was between my confessor and me." Andrée looked at me, her face serious. "You have to understand her," she said. "She's responsible for my soul: she can't always know what God wants of her either. It's not easy for anyone."

"No, it's not easy," I said vaguely.

I was furious. Madame Gallard tortured Andrée, and now *she* was the victim!

"Mama talked to me in a way that devastated me," said Andrée, filled with emotion. "She went through difficult times herself too, you know, when she was young." Andrée looked around her. "Right here, on these very paths, she had hard times."

"Was your grandmother very strict?"

"Yes."

Andrée was lost in thought for a moment.

"Mama says there are blessings, that God limits the tests He sends us, that He will help Bernard, and He'll help me the way He helped her."

She looked straight at me.

"Sylvie, if you don't believe in God, how can you bear to live?"

"But I like living," I said.

"So do I. But that's just it: if I thought that the people I love would die completely, I'd kill myself immediately."

"I don't want to kill myself," I said.

We had left the shade of the fig tree and gone back to the house in silence. Andrée took Communion the following Sunday.

CHAPTER 2

We took our baccalaureates, and after many long arguments, Madame Gallard allowed Andrée to spend three years studying at the Sorbonne. Andrée chose to major in literature, I in philosophy; we often worked side by side in the library, but I was alone in class. The language, behavior, and words of the students frightened me; I remained respectful of Christian morality, and I found the other students too liberal. It was no accident that I discovered I had things in common with Pascal Blondel, who had the reputation of being an observant Catholic. I appreciated his perfect upbringing and beautiful, angelic face as much as his intelligence. He smiled at all his friends but remained distant from everyone, and he seemed to be particularly wary of the women students, but my philosophical zeal overcame his reserve. We had long intellectual conversations, and all in all we agreed on almost every issue, apart from the existence of God. We decided to team up. Pascal detested public places, libraries, and cafés: I went to his place to work. The apartment he lived in with his father and sister resembled my parents' apartment, but the banality of his bedroom disappointed me. After I left the Adélaïde School, young men seemed to belong to a rather mysterious brotherhood that I imagined much more advanced than I was in the secrets of life, but Pascal's furniture, his books, the ivory crucifix, the El Greco reproduction, nothing indicated that he was a different species from Andrée and me. For a long time, he'd had the right to go out alone at night and to read whatever he pleased, but I quickly realized that his options were just as limited as mine. He'd been educated in a religious institution where his father was a teacher, and he loved only his studies and his family. At the time, all I thought about was getting away from home, and I was surprised that he felt so comfortable at his. He shook his head: "Never will I be as happy as I am now," he said, sounding as nostalgic as elderly men who missed the past. He told me that his father was a man to be admired. He had married late, after enduring a difficult childhood, and found himself a widower at the age of fifty with a little girl of ten and a baby who was a few months old; he had sacrificed himself entirely to them. As for his sister, Pascal considered her a saint. She had lost her fiancé during the war and decided she would never marry. Her chestnut-colored hair, pulled back into a heavy ponytail, revealed a high, intimidating forehead; she was very pale, with soulful eyes and a harsh, dazzling smile. She always wore the same style of dress: dark colors and elegantly austere, brightened up by a large white collar. She had energetically taken charge of her brother's education and had tried to steer him toward the priesthood. I suspected that she kept a private diary and imagined herself to be Eugénie de Guérin.* While darning the family's socks with her thick, rather ruddy hands, she must have been reciting Verlaine's words to herself: "The humble life, with boring, easy tasks." A good student, a good son, a good Christian, Pascal was a little too well behaved, I found; I sometimes thought that he seemed like a young unfrocked student from a seminary. On my side of things, I irritated him over more than one issue. And yet, even later on, when I had other friends who interested me more, our friendship held fast. He was the one I brought as my escort the day the Gallards were celebrating Malou's engagement.

Thanks to circling Napoleon's tomb, breathing in the scent of Bagatelle roses, and eating Russian salad in the forests of the Landes region, Malou, who then knew *Carmen*, *Manon*, and *Lakmé* by heart, finally found a husband. Every

---

* Eugénie de Guérin (1805–1848) was a French poet and diarist, the sister of the writer Maurice de Guérin, whom she attempted to lead into a religious life. [Trans.]

day since she had reached the age of twenty-five without being married, her mother had said, "Enter a convent or get married; celibacy is not a vocation." One evening, just as she was leaving for the Opéra, Madame Gallard had announced: "This time, you must take it or leave it. The next opportunity will be for Andrée." So Malou agreed to marry a widower who was forty years old and afflicted with two daughters. An afternoon tea dance was given to congratulate her. Andrée insisted that I come. I slipped on the gray silk dress my cousin had left to me after entering the convent and went to meet Pascal in front of the Gallards' house.

Monsieur Gallard had obtained an important promotion over the course of the past five years, and they now lived in a luxurious apartment on the Rue Marbeuf. I hardly ever set foot there. Madame Gallard said hello to me, reluctantly; for a long time now she no longer kissed me and didn't even bother to smile at me. However, she looked at Pascal without disapproval: all women liked him because he seemed simultaneously intense and reserved. Andrée gave him one of her standard smiles. She had rings under her eyes, and I wondered if she'd been crying. "If you want to freshen up your powder, you'll find everything you need in my room," she said. It was a discreet invitation. The Gallards allowed the use of powder, but my mother, her sisters, and her friends forbade it. "Makeup ruins the skin," they affirmed. My sisters and I often said that considering the sad state of their skin, the prudence of those ladies was hardly rewarded.

I smoothed my face with a powder puff, combed my badly cut hair, and went back into the living room. The youngsters danced under the tender eyes of the older women. It was not a pretty sight. Taffetas and satins in colors that were far too garish or sugary, boatneck dresses, awkwardly draped wraps, all these things made the young Christian women look even uglier, trained, as they were, to forget their bodies. Only Andrée was pleasant to look at. Her hair was lustrous, her nails shiny, she wore a long, pretty dark blue flowing dress and stiletto heels. Yet despite the circles of rouge she'd painted on her face to make herself look healthy, she seemed tired.

"It's so sad!" I said to Pascal.

"What is?"

"Everything!"

"No, it isn't," he said cheerfully.

Pascal shared neither my moments of harshness nor my rare enthusiasm; he said that in every living being, you could find something to love. That's why he pleased people so much: under his attentive gaze, everyone felt likable.

He asked me to dance, then I danced with other young men; they were all ugly. I had nothing to say to them and they had nothing to say to me; it was hot, I was bored. I kept close watch on Andrée; she smiled in the same way at all her dancing partners, greeted the old ladies with a little curtsy that was a bit too perfect for my liking. I didn't like seeing her so easily fulfill her role as a young lady of society. "Would she allow herself to be married off, like her sister?" I wondered, somewhat anxiously. A few months earlier, Andrée had run into Bernard in Biarritz, at the wheel of a long, pale blue car; he wore a white suit, had rings on his fingers, and was sitting beside a pretty blonde who was obviously a prostitute. They had shaken hands, having nothing to say. "Mama was right: we weren't meant for each other," Andrée had told me. Perhaps he would have been different if they hadn't been separated, I thought, but perhaps not. In any case, Andrée only ever spoke of love with bitterness after that.

Between two dances, I managed to walk over to her.

"Is there any way we could chat for five minutes?"

She touched her temple; she definitely had a headache, which happened to her often back then. "Meet you on the stairs, top floor. I'll find a way to sneak off." She glanced around at the couples who were changing partners. "Our mothers won't allow us to go for a walk with a young man, but they smile ecstatically when they see us dancing; they're so naive!"

Andrée often said bluntly, out loud, what I was quietly thinking to myself. Yes, these good Christian women should have been worried as they watched their daughters yielding, modestly, faces flushed, in a man's arms. How I had hated my dancing lessons when I was fifteen! I had a vague feeling of queasiness that resembled an upset stomach, weariness, sadness, though I could not understand why. After realizing what it meant, I became defiant; it seemed so irrational and annoying that anyone, simply through physical contact, could affect my feelings. But most of these prissy virgins certainly were more naive than I was, or at least had less self-esteem: now that I had started to think about it, I got annoyed watching them. "And what about Andrée?" I wondered. Her cynicism often forced me to ask myself questions that scandalized me the moment I thought of them. Andrée met me on the stairs; we sat down on the highest step.

"It feels good to have a little break!" she said.

"Do you have a headache?"

"Yes," said Andrée with a smile. "Maybe it's because of what I drank this morning. Normally, to get going, I drink some coffee or a glass of white wine: this morning I mixed the two."

"Coffee and wine?"

"It's not that bad. It was a real pick-me-up at the time." Andrée stopped smiling. "I didn't sleep at all last night. I'm so sad for Malou!"

Andrée had never gotten along well with her sister, but she took to heart everything that happened to people.

"Poor Malou!" she continued. "For two days, she ran

around asking all her friends what they thought; they all told her to say yes. Especially Guite," said Andrée, sniggering. "Guite said that after the age of twenty-eight, it's unbearable to spend your nights alone!"

"And spending them with a man you don't love is fun?" I asked, smiling. "Does Guite still believe in love at first sacrament?"

"I suppose," said Andrée, nervously playing with the gold chain that held her religious medals. "Oh! It's not that simple," she said. "*You'll* have a profession, you'll be able to fulfill some purpose without getting married. But a useless old maid like Guite, that's not good."

I often congratulated myself, egotistically, that the Bolsheviks and life's malevolence had ruined my father: I was obliged to work, the problems that tormented Andrée didn't concern me.

"Is it really impossible for them to let you study for the teaching diploma?"

"Impossible!" said Andrée. "Next year, I'll be taking Malou's place."

"And your mother will try to get you married?"

"I think it's already started," Andrée replied, laughing a little. "There's a young man from the Polytechnique who meticulously interrogates me about my tastes. I told him that I dreamed of caviar, designer clothes, and nightclubs—and that Louis Jouvet was my kind of man."

"Did he believe you?"

"He did at least seem worried."

We chatted for a few more minutes, then Andrée looked at her watch.

"I have to go back downstairs."

I hated that watch—her slave bracelet. Whenever we read in the library under the peaceful light of the green lamps, drank tea on the Rue Soufflot, or walked along the paths of the Luxembourg Gardens, Andrée would suddenly glance at her watch and flee in panic: "I'm late!" She always had something else to do: her mother burdened her with chores that she carried out with the zeal of a penitent. Andrée was obstinate in her love for her mother, and even if she was resigned to disobey her about certain things, it was only because her mother gave her no choice. Shortly after my visit to Béthary— Andrée was only fifteen then—Madame Gallard had told her about the birds and the bees with such intensity and minute detail that she still shuddered when thinking back on it. Afterward, her mother had calmly allowed her to read Lucretia, Boccaccio, Rabelais: coarse if not actually obscene works that did not upset her Christian mother. But Madame Gallard irrevocably condemned authors she accused of denigrating the Catholic religion and its morals. "If you want to learn about your religion, read the Church fathers," she'd say when she saw Andrée holding a book by Claudel, Mauriac, or Bernanos. She felt that I had a pernicious influence on Andrée and had wanted to forbid her from seeing me. Encouraged and guided by a teacher with more liberal ideas, Andrée had held fast. But to make amends for her studies, her reading, our friendship, she did her utmost to fulfill in an irreproachable manner what Madame Gallard called her social duties. That was why she had headaches so often. She hardly found time to practice the violin during the day; as for her classes, she could only barely manage to study at night, and even though she was very gifted, she didn't sleep enough.

Pascal often asked her to dance with him that afternoon.

"Your friend is very nice," he said earnestly, while accompanying me home. "I've seen you with her a lot at the Sorbonne: why didn't you ever introduce me to her?"

"It didn't occur to me," I said.

"I'd like to see her again."

"That would be easy."

I was surprised he admitted he was attracted to Andrée. He was friendly toward women, perhaps even a little more so than he was toward men, but he hardly seemed to hold women in esteem; despite his universal benevolence, he remained rather unsociable. As for Andrée, when seeing a new face, her first reaction was mistrust. As she grew up, she had discovered, with outrage, the chasm that separated the teaching of the Gospels and the self-serving, egotistical, petty behavior of self-righteous people; she defended herself against their hypocrisy by adopting a firm stance of cynicism. She believed me when I told her that Pascal was very intelligent, but even though she rebelled against stupidity, she attached little importance to intelligence. "What good is that?" she asked with a kind of annoyance. I didn't know exactly what she was looking for, but she used the same skepticism against all accepted values. If she happened to become infatuated with an artist, a writer, an actor, it was always for paradoxical reasons; she appreciated only their frivolous or even dubious qualities. Louis Jouvet had entranced her in a role as a drunkard to such an extent that she had hung his photograph up in her bedroom; these infatuations represented, above all, a challenge to the false virtues of respectable people; she didn't take them seriously. But she did seem serious when she spoke to me about Pascal: "I found him very nice."

And so, Pascal came and had tea with us on Rue Soufflot and accompanied us to the Luxembourg Gardens. After the second time, I left him alone with Andrée, and afterward, they often met without me. I wasn't jealous. Ever since that night in the kitchen in Béthary when I'd admitted to Andrée how much she meant to me, I had decided to make myself care about her a little less. She still counted enormously to me, but at present, there was the rest of the world, and myself: she was no longer everything.

Reassured to see Andrée finish her studies without having lost either her faith or her virtue, and satisfied to have married off her oldest daughter, Madame Gallard was more permissive throughout that entire spring. Andrée looked at her watch less often; she saw Pascal a lot alone, and the three of us often went out together. He quickly became an influence on her. He had begun by laughing at her sarcastic remarks and jaded jibes; but he soon reproached her for her pessimism. "Humanity is not so dark," he asserted. They discussed the problem of evil, sin, the state of grace, and he accused Andrée of Jansenism. She was very shocked by that. In the early days, she would be surprised and say, "He's so young!" Then, sounding perplexed, she'd say, "When I compare myself to Pascal, I have the impression that I'm a bitter old maid." She finally decided that he was the one who was right.

"Thinking badly of your equals a priori," she told me, "is to offend God." Then she continued: "A Christian must be fastidious, but not tormented. Pascal is the first true Christian I've ever met!" she added passionately.

Even more than Pascal's arguments, it was his very existence that reconciled Andrée with human nature, with the world, with God. He believed in heaven, and he loved life, he was cheerful and irreproachable: all of humanity was not bad after all, nor all virtues false, and you could reach paradise without renouncing the earthly world. I congratulated myself that Andrée allowed herself to be persuaded. Two years earlier, her faith had seemed to waver: "There is only one type of faith possible," she'd told me then, "and that is blind faith." Afterward, she'd changed her thinking. All I could hope was that she didn't have too cruel an idea of religion. Pascal, who shared her beliefs, was better placed than I was to assure her that it wasn't criminal to sometimes think about yourself. Without condemning Madame Gallard, he confirmed to Andrée that she'd been right to stand up for her personal life. "God does not want us to demean ourselves and become like animals: if He has granted us His gifts, it's so that we will use them," he often told her. These words filled Andrée with enthusiasm; you would have thought that an enormous weight had been lifted from her shoulders. As the chestnut trees in the Luxembourg Gardens were covered in buds, then leaves and flowers, I watched her transform. In her flannel suit, straw cloche hat, and gloves, she had the reserved appearance of a respectable young woman. Pascal gently teased her.

"Why do you always wear hats that hide your face? Do you ever take off your gloves? Is it possible to suggest to such a proper person that they sit down outside a café?"

She looked happy when he teased her. She didn't buy a new hat, but she left her gloves at the bottom of her handbag and sat outside the cafés on the Boulevard Saint-Michel; the way she carried herself once more became as lively as when we used to go for walks beneath the pine trees. Up until then, Andrée's beauty had remained more or less a secret: it existed deep in her eyes, suddenly flashing across her face for an instant, but was never completely visible. Suddenly, her beauty rose to the surface, burst into view. I can remember her one morning and the scent of fresh grass on the lake in the Bois de Boulogne. She had taken the oars; with no hat, no gloves, and bare arms, she skillfully parted the water. Her hair was shiny, her eyes alive. Pascal let his hand drift through the water as he softly sang a song: he had a nice voice and knew a lot of songs.

He too was changing. In front of his father and especially his sister, he seemed like a very young boy; but he spoke to Andrée with the authority of a man. Not that he was playing a role: he simply rose to her need of him. Or perhaps I hadn't really known him, or maybe he was maturing. In any case, he no longer seemed like a young man from the seminary. I found him less angelic than in the past, but more cheerful; and cheerfulness became him. On the afternoon of May 1, he was waiting for us in front of the Luxembourg Gardens; when he saw us, he climbed onto the balustrade and headed toward us, taking the tiny steps of a tightrope walker, using his arms to steady himself. In each hand, he held a bouquet of lilies of the valley. He jumped down and held them out to both of us at the same time. My flowers were just there for symmetry: Pascal had never given me flowers. Andrée understood, because she blushed: it was the second time in our lives that I had seen her blush. "They love each other," I thought. It was a very lucky thing to be loved by Andrée; but I was especially overjoyed for her. She would not have been able, or have wanted, to marry someone who wasn't a believer; if she had resigned herself to loving an austere Christian, like Monsieur Gallard, she would have died. With Pascal, she could finally reconcile her duty and her happiness.

At the end of that year, we didn't have very much to do; we wandered around a lot. None of us was rich. Madame Gallard allowed her daughters only enough pocket money to buy bus tickets and stockings; Monsieur Blondel wanted Pascal to dedicate himself exclusively to his exams, he forbade him from giving private lessons, preferring to take on the burden of more hours of work himself; and I had only two students who paid very little. We still managed, however, to go to the Ursulines movie theater to watch intellectual films and avant-garde plays in the theaters of the Cartel des Quatre.* When we came out, I always had long discussions with Andrée. Pascal would listen with an air of indulgence. He claimed he loved nothing but

---

* The "Cartel des Quatre" was formed in 1927 by four famous directors working in the Paris theater: Louis Jouvet, Charles Dullin, Gaston Baty, and Georges Pitoëff. [Trans.]

philosophy. Art and literature, deemed gratuitous, bored him; but when they claimed to represent life, he judged them as false. He said that in reality, feelings and situations were not as subtle or dramatic as in books. Andrée found this simplistic attitude refreshing. Basically, she tended to see the world as too tragic, so it was better for her that Pascal's wisdom was rather limited but optimistic.

After her oral exam, which she passed brilliantly, Andrée left to go for a walk with Pascal. He never invited her to his place, and she undoubtedly would not have agreed to go: without going into precise detail, she told her mother that she was going out with me and some other friends, but she would not have wished to either admit or hide that she had spent the afternoon at the home of a young man. They always saw each other outside and went for many walks.

I met her the next day in our usual spot, beneath the cold expression of the stone statue of a queen. I'd bought some cherries, the fat black cherries she liked, but she refused to taste them; she seemed worried. After a moment, she spoke: "I talked to Pascal about what happened between me and Bernard." Her voice was tense.

"You'd never told him about it?"

"No. I've wanted to for a long time. I felt I had to talk to him about it, but I didn't dare." She hesitated. "I was afraid he'd think very badly of me."

"But why!" I said.

Even though I'd known Andrée for ten years, she often mystified me.

"Bernard and I never did anything wrong," she said in a serious voice, "but we did kiss, and they weren't platonic kisses. Pascal is so pure. I was afraid he'd be terribly shocked." Then she added with conviction: "But he's only harsh with himself."

"How could he have been shocked?" I said. "You and Bernard were children, and you loved each other."

"You can sin at any age," said Andrée, "and love doesn't excuse everything."

"Pascal must have found you very Jansenistic!" I said.

I didn't understand her scruples very well; it's also true that I didn't realize exactly what those childlike kisses meant to her.

"He understood," she said. "He always understands everything." She looked around her. "And to think that I thought about killing myself when Mama separated me from Bernard: I was so sure I'd love him forever!" There was a nervous hesitation in her voice.

"At fifteen, it's normal to make mistakes," I said.

Andrée traced lines in the sand with the tips of her shoes. "How old do you have to be before you have the right to think: this is forever?"

Her face hardened when she was worried, it looked almost skeletal.

"You're not making a mistake now," I said.

"That's what I think too," she said. She continued drawing wavy lines on the ground. "But what about the other person, the one you love, how can you be sure he'll love you forever?"

"You must be able to sense it," I said.

She pulled a few cherries out of the brown paper bag and ate them in silence.

"Pascal told me that until now, he'd never been in love with any woman," Andrée said.

She looked straight at me.

"He didn't say, 'I'd never loved,' he said, 'I have never loved.'"

I smiled. "Pascal is scrupulous; he weighs his words."

"He asked me if we could take Communion together tomorrow morning," said Andrée.

I didn't reply. I thought that if I were Andrée, I would have been jealous seeing Pascal take Communion; a human being is so insignificant compared to God. Yet it's true that in the past, I had felt tremendous love for both Andrée and God at the same time.

From that point on, it was understood by Andrée and me that she loved Pascal. As for him, he spoke to her more confidently than in the past. He told her that between the ages of sixteen and eighteen, he had wanted to become a priest. His sister had encouraged him, but his spiritual adviser had shown him that it wasn't his true vocation. What he was seeking at the seminary was a refuge from the outside world and the adult responsibilities that frightened him. That fear had persisted for a long time and explained Pascal's prejudices where women were concerned: at present, he reproached himself severely. "Purity does not consist in seeing every woman as harboring a devil," he cheerfully told Andrée. Before meeting her, he had made an exception only for his sister, whom he considered a pure spirit, and for me, because I had such little awareness of being a woman. He now understood that women were, in their capacity as women, God's creatures. "However, there is only one Andrée in the world," he'd added, and with so much warmth that she no longer doubted that he loved her.

"Will you write to each other over the summer vacation?" I asked Andrée.

"Yes."

"What will Madame Gallard say?"

"Mama never opens my letters," said Andrée, "and she'll have other things to do besides keeping an eye on the mail."

The summer was going to be particularly hectic because of Malou's engagement; Andrée talked about it to me with a sense of apprehension.

"Would you come," she asked me, "if Mama let me invite you?"

"She won't let you," I said.

"That's not definite. Mine and Lélette will be in England, and the twins are too young for you to be a dangerous influence," Andrée said, laughing. "Mama trusts me now," she added in a serious tone of voice. "I've had difficult moments but ended up by earning her trust: she's no longer afraid you'll corrupt me."

I suspected that Andrée wanted me to come not simply because of our friendship, but because she could talk to me about Pascal; I couldn't have asked for anything better than to be the one she confided in, and I was very happy when Andrée told me she was counting on me at the beginning of September.

DURING THE MONTH OF AUGUST, I received only two very short letters from Andrée; she wrote from her bed, at dawn. "During the day, I don't have a minute to myself," she said. She was sleeping in a room with her grandmother, who was a light sleeper; to write letters or read, she waited until the light slipped through the shutters on the window. The house at Béthary was full of people; there was the fiancé and his two sisters, frail old maids who didn't let Andrée out of their sight, as well as their Rivière de Bonneuil cousins. While celebrating Malou's engagement, Madame Gallard was still organizing meetings with prospective suitors for Andrée; it was a hectic summer with one party followed by the next. "This is how I imagine hell," Andrée wrote to me. In September, she had to accompany Malou to visit her fiancé's parents: the very thought of it depressed her. Fortunately, she was getting long letters from Pascal. I couldn't wait to see her. That year, I was bored in Sadernac; solitude weighed heavily on me.

Andrée was waiting for me on the platform, wearing a pink toile dress and a straw cloche hat. But she wasn't alone: the twins, one dressed in pink gingham, the other in blue gingham, were running toward the train, shouting: "There's Sylvie! Hello, Sylvie!"

With their straight hair and dark eyes, they reminded me of the little girl whose thigh had been burnt to a crisp, and who had won my heart, ten years before; except their cheeks were rounder, their expressions less insolent. Andrée smiled at me; it was a brief smile but so vivacious that she seemed glowing with good health.

"Did you have a good journey?" she asked, holding out her hand.

"I always do when I travel alone," I said.

The little girls watched us.

"Why don't you give her a kiss," the blue twin asked Andrée, as if criticizing us.

"There are people whom you love a lot but don't kiss," said Andrée.

"There are people whom you kiss but don't even like," said the pink twin.

"Exactly," said Andrée. "Take Sylvie's suitcase to the car," she added.

The little girls grabbed my case and skipped over to the black Citroën parked in front of the station.

"How are things?" I asked Andrée.

"Not good, not bad: I'll fill you in," said Andrée.

She slipped in behind the wheel and I sat down next to her; the twins got into the backseat, which was full of packages. It was clear that I'd landed in the middle of an extremely regimented life. "Before picking up Sylvie, you'll do the shopping and go and get the girls," Madame Gallard had said. When we arrived, we'd have to unpack them all. Andrée put on her gloves and shifted gears. When I looked at her more closely, I realized she was thinner.

"You've lost weight," I said.

"Maybe, a little."

"She has," shouted one of the twins, "Mama tells her off, but she doesn't eat a thing."

"She doesn't eat a thing," the other one repeated.

"Don't say such silly things," said Andrée. "If I didn't eat a thing, I'd be dead."

The car slowly began to move. The gloved hands on the steering wheel looked competent: besides, everything Andrée did, she did well.

"Do you like to drive?"

"I don't like playing chauffeur all day long, but I do like driving."

The car continued down the road lined with locust trees, but I didn't recognize it; the steep hill where Madame Gallard had to use the brakes, the incline where the horse took slow, heavy steps, all of it had been flattened. And we were already coming to the wide avenue. The box trees were newly trimmed. The château hadn't changed, but borders of begonias and enormous zinnias had been planted in front of the main entrance.

"These flowers weren't here before," I said.

"No. They're ugly," said Andrée, "but now that we have a gardener, we have to keep him busy," she added sarcastically.

She took my suitcase. "Tell Mama I'll be right there," she said to the twins.

I recognized the entrance hall and how it smelled like the countryside. The steps on the staircase creaked as before, but, on the landing, Andrée turned left. "You've been put in the twins' room; they'll sleep with Grandmother and me."

Andrée pushed open a door and put my suitcase down on the floor. "Mama claims that if we're in the same room, we won't sleep a wink all night."

"That's a shame!" I said.

"Yes. But at least it's good that you're here!" said Andrée. "I'm so happy about that!"

"Me too."

"Come down as soon as you're ready," she said. "I have to go help Mama."

She closed the door. She wasn't exaggerating when she wrote to me saying, "I don't have a minute to myself." Andrée never exaggerated. But she'd found the time to pick three red roses for me, her favorite flowers. I remembered something she'd written as a child: "I like roses; they are ceremonial flowers that die without fading, in a curtsy." I opened the wardrobe to hang up my only dress; it was a pale mauve color. Inside, I found a robe, slippers, and a pretty white dress with red polka dots. On the dressing table, Andrée had set out a bar of almond soap, a bottle of cologne, and some powder, in the shade called "Rachel." Her concern for me was touching.

"Why isn't she eating?" I wondered. Perhaps Madame Gallard had intercepted her letters: why should that matter? Five years had passed: was the same story about to start over again? I left my room and went down the stairs. It wouldn't be the same story; Andrée was no longer a child. I sensed, I *knew*, that she loved Pascal with an undying love. I reassured myself by telling myself over and over again that Madame Gallard would find nothing to object to if they married. All in all, Pascal could be categorized as "a young man suitable in all respects."

A loud din of voices was coming from the living room;

the idea of facing all those somewhat hostile people intimidated me: I wasn't a child anymore either. I went into the library to wait for the dinner bell to ring. I remembered the books, the photographs, the heavy photo album with the embossed leather cover decorated in garlands and bands, like the ones used in the ceiling moldings; I unfastened the metal clasp. My eyes were drawn to the photograph of Madame Rivière de Bonneuil: at fifty, with her straight dark hair coiled around her head and her authoritarian expression, she did not resemble the sweet grandmother she'd become; she had forced her daughter to marry a man she hadn't wanted. I turned over several pages of the photo album and looked closely at the picture of Madame Gallard as a young woman. A high-necked blouse constricted her neck, her fluffy hair sat on top of a naive face, and her mouth looked the same as Andrée's, full and severe and unsmiling; there was something attractive about her expression. I found her again a little farther on, sitting next to a young man with a beard, and smiling at an ugly baby; the "something attractive" I'd found before in her eyes had disappeared. I closed the photo album, walked over to the French window, and opened it; a breeze was rustling through the money plant and murmuring among its delicate seed heads. The swing creaked. "She was our age," I thought. She listened to the whispering night under the same stars and made a promise to herself: "No, I won't marry him." Why? He wasn't ugly or stupid, he had a good future and many virtues. Did she love someone else? Did she have dreams for herself? Today she seemed perfectly suited to the life she'd led!

The dinner bell rang, and I went down to the dining room. I shook a lot of hands, but no one took the time to ask anything about me, and I was quickly forgotten. Throughout the whole meal, Charles and Henri Rivière de Bonneuil loudly defended *L'action française* and the newspaper's stance against the pope, whom Monsieur Gallard supported. Andrée looked annoyed. As for Madame Gallard, she was obviously thinking of other things; I tried in vain to find a trace of the young woman from the photo album on her washed-out face. "Yet she has memories," I thought. "What kind? And what does she make of them?"

After dinner, the men played bridge and the women got back to their crafts. That year, paper hats were all the rage: thick paper was cut into thin strips that were dampened to make them more flexible; they were then tightly interwoven and coated all over with a kind of varnish. Under the admiring gaze of the Santenay ladies, Andrée was making something green.

"Will that be a cloche hat?" I asked.

"No, a big wide-brimmed hat," she said with a knowing smile.

Agnès Santenay asked her to play the violin, but Andrée refused. I realized that I wasn't going to be able to speak to her at all that evening, so I went up to bed early. I didn't see her alone for a single minute during the days that followed. In the morning, she did chores in the house; in the afternoon, all the youngsters piled into Monsieur Gallard's and Charles's cars to play tennis or go dancing at one of the châteaux in the area, or we'd be dropped off in some small village to watch a tournament of Basque pelota or other kinds of games unique to the Landes region.* Andrée laughed when she was supposed to. But I noticed that she was, in fact, eating hardly anything at all.

One night, I woke up when I heard someone opening the door to my bedroom.

"Sylvie, are you asleep?"

Andrée came over to my bed; she was barefoot and wrapped in a fleece robe.

"What time is it?"

"One o'clock. If you're not too sleepy, let's go downstairs; it will be easier to talk down there. People might hear us up here."

I slipped on my bathrobe and we went downstairs,

---

* The reference here is to the "Course des vaches," a kind of nonviolent bullfight in which cows whose horns had been filed down charged at the young men. [Trans.]

avoiding the steps that creaked. Andrée went into the library and switched on a lamp.

"Every other night, I never managed to get out of bed without waking Grandmother up. It's unbelievable what light sleepers old people are."

"I've been dying to talk to you," I said.

"Me too!" Andrée sighed. "It's been this hard since the beginning of the summer. I've had such bad luck: I so wanted everyone to leave me the hell alone this year!"

"Does your mother suspect anything yet?" I asked.

"Unfortunately!" said Andrée. "She finally noticed the envelopes with a man's handwriting. Last week she questioned me about it." She shrugged. "In any case, I was going to have to talk to her about him one day or another."

"Well? What did she say?"

"I told her everything," said Andrée. "She didn't ask to see Pascal's letters, and I wouldn't have shown them to her; but I did tell her everything. She didn't forbid me from continuing to write to him. She said she needed some time to think it over."

Andrée glanced around the room, as if trying to find something to help her; the austere-looking books and portraits of her ancestors were not the kinds of things to reassure her.

"Did she seem very annoyed? When will you know what she's decided?"

"I have no idea," said Andrée. "She didn't comment, just asked questions. Then said rather dryly, 'I have to think it over.'"

"There's no reason at all for her to object to Pascal," I said heatedly. "Even from her point of view, it's not a bad match."

"I don't know. In our social circle, marriages don't happen like this," said Andrée. "A love match is suspicious," she added bitterly.

"Still, they won't prevent you from marrying Pascal simply because you love him!"

"I don't know," Andrée said again, sounding vague. She glanced quickly at me, then looked away. "I don't even know if Pascal thinks about marrying me," she said.

"Come on now! He hasn't talked to you about marriage because it goes without saying. To Pascal, loving you and wanting to marry you are the same thing," I said.

"He never told me he loves me," said Andrée.

"I know. But recently, in Paris, you were sure he does," I said. "And you were quite right: it was completely obvious."

Andrée started fiddling with the medals on her necklace; she remained silent for a moment.

"In my first letter, I told Pascal that I loved him. Maybe I was wrong, but I don't know how to explain it to you: keeping silent seemed like a lie in a letter."

I nodded; Andrée had always been incapable of deception.

"He replied with a very beautiful letter," said Andrée. "But he said he didn't feel he had the right to use the word 'love.' He explained that in his worldly life as in his religious life, he had never had any certainty: he needs to test his feelings."

"Don't worry," I said. "Pascal always reproached me for deciding what my opinions were instead of putting them to the test: that's how he is! He needs to take his time. But his experiment will quickly be conclusive."

I knew Pascal well enough to know he wasn't playing games; but I hated his reticence. Andrée would have slept better, eaten more, if she'd been assured of his love.

"Did you tell him about your conversation with Madame Gallard?"

"Yes," said Andrée.

"You'll see: as soon as he fears your relationship is in danger, he'll be sure."

Andrée was biting on one of her medals.

"I'll wait and see," she said, without much conviction.

"Honestly, Andrée, do you really believe that Pascal could love another woman?"

She hesitated. "He might realize that he does not have a vocation for marriage."

"You don't imagine that he's still thinking about becoming a priest!"

"He might still have thought about it if he hadn't met

me," said Andrée. "Perhaps I'm a trap put on his path to turn him away from his true calling . . ."

I looked at Andrée and felt worried. She was a Jansenist, Pascal had said, but it was worse: she suspected God of diabolical conspiracies.

"That's absurd," I said. "In a pinch, I could imagine God might tempt souls, but not deceive them."

Andrée shrugged. "People say you have to have faith because believing is irrational. So I end up thinking that the more irrational things seem, the more likely they are to be true."

We'd been talking for a while when suddenly the library door opened.

"What are you doing in here?" asked a little voice.

It was Dédé, the twin in pink, the one Andrée preferred.

"Well, what about you?" said Andrée. "Why aren't you in bed?"

Dédé walked over to us, holding up her long white nightgown.

"Grandma woke me up when she turned on the lamp; she asked me where you were: I said I'd go and see . . ."

Andrée stood up. "Be a good girl. I'm going to tell Grandmother that I couldn't sleep so I came down to the library to read. Don't say anything about Sylvie: Mama will scold me."

"But that's a lie," said Dédé.

"I'm the one who will lie, all you have to do is say nothing; you won't be telling a lie. When you're big, you're sometimes allowed to lie," Andrée added, reassuring her.

"It's convenient being big," said Dédé with a sigh.

"Sometimes, sometimes not," said Andrée, stroking her head.

"How tyrannical!" I thought as I went back to my bedroom. Every one of her actions was controlled by her mother, or her grandmother, and automatically became an example to her little sisters. She couldn't have a single thought that wasn't accountable to God!

"That's the worst part," I thought the next day, while Andrée was praying next to me on a pew where a brass nameplate had reserved it for the Rivière de Bonneuils for over a century. Madame Gallard was holding a harmonium; the twins were walking up and down the church with baskets full of consecrated bread. Andrée, her head in her hands, was talking to God: what was she saying? She couldn't have had a simple relationship with Him. I was certain of one thing: she had not managed to convince herself that He was good, yet she didn't want to displease Him and was trying to love Him. Things would have been simpler if she had lost her faith, like me, as soon as her faith had lost its naivete. I watched the twins. They were busy and important; at their age, religion is a very amusing game. I had waved banners and thrown rose petals before the priest dressed in gold who carried the Eucharist; I had joined the parade in my Communion dress and kissed large amethyst rings on the hands of bishops; velvety monstrances, altars in the month of the Virgin Mary, nativity scenes, displays, angels, incense, all those scents, ritualized activities, brilliant trappings—those things had been the only luxuries of my childhood. And how pleasant it all was, being in awe of so much magnificence, feeling within oneself a soul as pure and radiant as the Host at the heart of the monstrance! And then, one day, the soul and the heavens become enveloped in darkness, and you find, lodged deep within yourself, remorse, sin, fear. Even when she limited herself to considering the worldly aspects, Andrée took everything that happened around her terribly seriously. How could she not be filled with anguish when she imagined her life in the mysterious light of the supernatural world? Defying her mother was perhaps her way of revolting against God Himself: but perhaps by rebelling, she was proving herself unworthy of the blessings she had received. How could she know if, by loving Pascal, she wasn't serving Satan's schemes? At every instant, blessed eternity was in play, and no clear sign was given to indicate if you were about to achieve it or lose it! Pascal had helped Andrée overcome those terrors. But our conversation that night had shown me that she might easily fall back into their grip. It was certainly not at church that she found peace in her heart.

I was depressed the whole afternoon and watched gloomily as the cows charged at terrified young men. For the next three days, all the women in the house were continually busy in the cellars; I even shelled peas and took the pits out of plums. Every year, all the wealthy landowners in the area got together on the banks of the Adour River to picnic on cold food; this innocent feast demanded time-consuming preparations. "Every family wants to outdo all the others and, every year, do better than the last," Andrée told me. The morning of the feast, they filled a rented van with two baskets stuffed with food and dishes; the youngsters piled into whatever space was left; the older ones and the engaged couples followed in cars. I'd put on the red polka-dot dress Andrée had loaned me; she was wearing a raw silk dress with a green belt that matched her big hat, which you could hardly tell was made of paper.

Blue water, old oak trees, thick grass; we would lie down in the grass, eat a sandwich, talk until evening: an afternoon of perfect happiness, I told myself gloomily as I helped Andrée unpack the baskets and hampers. What a fuss! We had to put up the tables, spread out the tablecloths in the right places, set out the food. Other cars arrived: two brand-new, shiny cars; a few antique jalopies, and even a carriage with two horses. The young people immediately started to pull out the dishes. The elderly ones sat down on tree trunks covered with tarpaulins or on folding chairs. Andrée greeted them with smiles and curtsies: she was particularly liked by the middle-aged men, with whom she spoke for a long time. In between, she took over from Malou and Guite, who were turning the handle of a complicated piece of equipment that had been filled with cream; they were trying to make ice cream. I helped them too.

"Can you believe it!" I said, pointing to the tables covered with food.

"Yes, all the best Christians must carry out their social obligations!" said Andrée.

The cream wouldn't thicken. We gave up and sat down around one of the tablecloths, joining the group of young people who were over twenty. Cousin Charles was speaking in a sophisticated tone of voice to a very ugly young woman who was wearing wonderful clothes: no words seemed adequate to describe the color or fabric of her dress.

"This picnic looks like a ball with green trimmings," murmured Andrée.

"Is it a meeting with a prospective suitor?" I said. "The girl's really ugly."

"But really rich," said Andrée, sniggering: there were at least ten marriages being arranged.

At the time, I was rather insatiable when it came to food, but the abundance and solemnity of the dishes being passed around by the servants put me off. Fish in jelly, in cones, in aspic or shaped pastry, galantines, stuffed meats, casseroles, cold meats in sauce, pâtés, terrines, preserved goose and duck, duck breast cooked in wine sauce, cold vegetable salads, plain and in mayonnaise, pies, tarts, and almond cakes: you had to taste it all and compliment everything so you didn't offend anyone. And on top of that, everyone talked about what they were eating. Andrée had a better appetite than usual, and at the beginning of the meal, she was rather cheerful. The man on her right, a handsome snob with dark hair, continually tried to get her attention and spoke to her in a low voice; she soon seemed irritated. Anger, or the wine, made her cheeks turn a bit pink; all the winegrowers had brought samples of their wines, and we emptied many bottles.

The conversation grew lively. We got around to talking about flirting: were we allowed to flirt? And how much? On the whole, everyone was against it, but it gave the boys and girls a chance to snigger and whisper together. All in all, these young people were rather straitlaced; some of them, however, clearly made a bad impression: there was a lot of bawdy snickering. The titillated young men began telling stories, respectful ones, but in a tone of voice that suggested they could have been telling different ones. They opened a magnum of champagne, and someone suggested that we all drink from the same glass so that we would learn the thoughts of our neighbor; the flute was passed around. After a handsome, smug young man had taken a drink, he handed the glass to Andrée and whispered something in her ear; she slapped it out of his hand, flinging it onto the grass.

"I don't like people getting too familiar," she said firmly.

There was an embarrassed silence, then Charles burst out laughing. "Our Andrée doesn't want us to know her secrets?"

"I don't want to know anyone else's," she said. "Besides, I've already had too much to drink." Standing up, she said, "I'm going to get some coffee."

I watched her, confused. I would have taken a drink without making a fuss; yes, there was something troubling in these innocent innuendos, but what did that have to do with us? Undoubtedly, to Andrée, it was sacrilegious, this artificial meeting of two mouths on a glass: was she thinking of Bernard and how they used to kiss, or of Pascal and the kisses he hadn't yet given her? Andrée didn't come back; I also stood up and headed for the shade of the oak trees. Once again, I wondered what exactly she meant when she spoke of kisses that were not platonic. I was very well informed about sexual issues, for during my childhood and adolescence, my body had had its desires, but neither my considerable wisdom nor my infinitesimal experience could explain the ties that united the flesh to tenderness, or happiness. To Andrée, there existed a link between the heart and the body that remained a mystery to me.

I emerged from the thicket. I found myself on the bank at the curve of the Adour River; I could hear the sound of a waterfall. At the bottom of the clear water, the mottled pebbles looked like bonbons posing as little stones.

"Sylvie!"

It was Madame Gallard, her face bright red beneath her straw hat.

"Do you know where Andrée is?"

"I was looking for her," I said.

"It's been nearly an hour since she disappeared; it's very rude."

In truth, I said to myself, she's worried. Perhaps Madame Gallard did love Andrée in her own way: but in which way? That was the question. We all loved her in our own way.

The sound of the waterfall was pounding loudly in our ears.

"I was sure of it!" said Madame Gallard, stopping.

Under a tree, near a cluster of autumn crocuses, I could make out Andrée's dress, her green belt, her heavy cotton slip. Madame Gallard walked closer to the river: "Andrée!"

Something moved at the foot of the waterfall.

"Come in!" said Andrée, peeking her head out. "The water is marvelous!"

"Come out of there immediately!"

Andrée swam toward us, her face lit up with laughter.

"And just after lunch! You could have gotten cramps!" said Madame Gallard.

Andrée hauled herself onto the riverbank; she had wrapped herself up in a woolen cape that she adjusted with some pins; the water had straightened her hair, and it fell over her eyes.

"Oh! Just look at you!" said Madame Gallard, in a gentler voice. "How are you going to get dry?"

"I'll manage."

"I do wonder what the Good Lord was thinking when He gave me such a daughter!" said Madame Gallard. She was smiling, but added quite harshly: "Come back immediately. You're failing in all your duties."

"I'm coming."

Madame Gallard walked away, and I sat down on the other side of the tree while Andrée got dressed.

"Oh!" she said. "I felt so good in the water!"

"It must have been ice-cold."

"When I first felt the waterfall on my back, it took my breath away," said Andrée, "but it did feel good."

I picked an autumn crocus. I wondered if they really were poisonous, these odd flowers that were both rustic and sophisticated in their simplicity, flowers that sprang from the earth in a single burst, like mushrooms.

"Do you think the Santenay sisters would die if we had them drink a soup made from these autumn crocuses?" I asked.

"Those poor girls!" said Andrée. "They're not really that bad."

She came over to me; she'd put her dress on and was adjusting the belt.

"I dried myself with my slip," she said. "No one will see that I'm not wearing a slip; we always wear too many clothes." She spread out the damp cape and crumpled skirt on the grass. "We have to go back."

"Too bad!"

"Poor Sylvie! You must be really bored." She smiled at me. "Now that the picnic is over, I hope I'll have more free time."

"Do you think you could manage to arrange for us to see each other a little?"

"One way or the other, I'll arrange it," she said, sounding determined.

As we were slowly walking back along the riverbank, she said: "I got a letter from Pascal this morning."

"A good letter?"

She nodded. "Yes." She crumpled some mint leaves in her hand and breathed in the scent; she seemed happy.

"He said that if Mama asked for time to think about it, that's a good sign," she continued. "He said that I should be confident."

"That's what I think too."

"I *am* confident," said Andrée.

I wanted to ask her why she had thrown the champagne glass on the ground, but I was afraid to embarrass her.

For the rest of the day, Andrée was charming with everyone; but I was hardly having a good time. And during the days that followed, she had no more free time than before. No doubt whatsoever: Madame Gallard intentionally arranged things so we wouldn't see each other. When she discovered Pascal's letters, she must have been kicking herself for having allowed me to visit, and she was making up for her mistake as best she could. And I was even sadder because the time was nearing when I had to say goodbye. When they returned, there would be Malou's wedding, I told myself that morning, and Andrée would replace her sister at home and in society; I'd get a glimpse of her in a rush between some charity sale and a funeral.

It was two days before my departure and, as often happened, I walked around the grounds while everyone was still asleep. Summer was dying, the shrubs were changing color, the red berries on the mountain ash trees were turning yellow; beneath the pale morning breeze, the copper colors of autumn seemed more intense. I liked seeing the trees shimmering brightly above the grass, still covered in dew from the cold. As I sadly walked along the well-kept pathways where wildflowers no longer grew, I thought I could hear music. I walked toward it; it was the sound of a violin. At the very end of the grounds, hidden within a cluster of pine trees, Andrée was playing. She'd thrown an old shawl over her blue jersey dress and was listening, thoughtfully, to the voice of the instrument propped against her shoulder. Her beautiful black hair fell to one side; the neat line made by the part was so moving that I wanted to run my fingers along it with tenderness and respect. I secretly watched the bow flow back and forth for a moment and thought, looking at Andrée, "She's so alone!"

As the final note faded away, I walked over to her, my footsteps crunching the pine needles.

"Oh!" said Andrée. "Did you hear me playing? Can they hear me at the house?"

"No," I said. "I was taking a walk. You play so well!" I added.

Andrée sighed. "If only I had some time to practice!"

"Do you often hold outdoor concerts like this?"

"No. But I've wanted to play so much these past few days! And I don't want all those people to hear me."

Andrée lay her violin in its little case.

"I have to get back before Mama comes downstairs; she'll say that I'm mad, and that won't help matters for me."

"Are you bringing your violin to the Santenays'?" I asked as we headed back to the house.

"Absolutely not! Oh! Spending time there horrifies me." She added, "At least here, I feel at home."

"Are you really obliged to go?"

"I don't want to fight with Mama over little things," she said. "Especially not now."

"I understand," I said.

Andrée went back into the house, and I sat down in the middle of the lawn with a book. A little later, I saw her cutting roses with the Santenay sisters. Then she went to chop some wood in the shed; I could hear the dull sound of the ax.

The sun was rising in the sky, and I found no pleasure in reading. I was no longer at all sure that Madame Gallard's decision might be favorable. Andrée would have only a small dowry, like her sister, but she was much prettier and far more brilliant than Malou; her mother undoubtedly nurtured high hopes for her. Suddenly, there was a loud cry: it was Andrée.

I ran toward the woodshed. Madame Gallard was leaning over her; Andrée was lying in the sawdust, her eyes closed, one foot bleeding. The blade of the ax was streaked with red.

"Malou, bring down your first-aid kit, Andrée is hurt!" cried Madame Gallard. She asked me to go and phone the doctor. When I came back, Malou was bandaging Andrée's foot, and her mother was making her breathe smelling salts.

"I dropped the ax!" she whispered, opening her eyes.

"The bone hasn't been cut," said Malou. "It's a deep gash, but the bone wasn't touched."

Andrée had a mild fever, and the doctor found she was very tired; he ordered her to rest for a long time. In any case, she wouldn't be able to walk on that foot for nearly two weeks.

When I went to see her that evening, she was very pale, but she gave me a big smile.

"I'm laid up until the end of the summer holidays!" she said in a triumphant voice.

"Are you in pain?" I asked.

"Not much!" she said. "Even if it hurt ten times as much, I'd prefer that to going to the Santenays'," she added. She looked at me mischievously. "It's what's called a happy accident!"

I stared at her, confused. "Andrée! You didn't really do this on purpose?"

"I couldn't hope that fate would be bothered with such a small thing," she said cheerfully.

"How did you have the courage! You could have cut off your foot!"

Andrée leaned back, her head against the pillow. "I couldn't stand it anymore," she said.

She looked up at the ceiling for a moment in silence, and seeing her chalk-white face, her blank expression, I could feel an old fear rising up again within me. Raise the ax, strike: I would *never* have been capable of that, the very idea repulsed me.

What terrified me was what she had been thinking just as she'd done it.

"Does your mother suspect?"

"I don't think so," she said, sitting up in bed. "I told you I'd find a way to have some peace, one way or another."

"You'd already decided?"

"I'd decided to do something. The idea of the ax came to me this morning while picking flowers. I first thought of cutting myself with the shears, but that wouldn't have been enough."

"You frighten me," I said.

Andrée gave me a big smile.

"Why? I did a good job: I didn't cut too deep. Do you want me to ask Mama if you can stay until the end of the month?" she added.

"She won't want me to."

"Let me talk to her!"

Did Madame Gallard suspect the truth? Did it make

her feel fear and remorse? Or was it the doctor's diagnosis that worried her? She agreed to have me stay in Béthary to keep Andrée company. The Rivière de Bonneuils left at the same time as Malou and the Santenays; overnight, the house grew very calm.

Andrée had her own room, and I spent many long hours at her bedside.

"I had a very long conversation with Mama about Pascal," she said to me one morning.

"And?"

Andrée lit a cigarette; she smoked whenever she was nervous.

"She had a chat with Papa. A priori, they have nothing against Pascal; he even made a good impression on them the day you brought him to the house."

Andrée looked straight at me. "It's just, I understand Mama: she doesn't know Pascal and she wonders if his intentions are serious."

"She wouldn't oppose a marriage?" I asked, full of hope.

"No."

"Well! That's what's most important," I said. "Aren't you happy?"

Andrée took a puff of her cigarette. "There would be no question of marriage for two or three years . . ."

"I know."

"Mama is demanding that we get officially engaged.

Otherwise, she has forbidden me to see Pascal: she wants to send me to England, to sever all contact."

"So you'll get engaged, that's all." Then I quickly added, "Okay, you've never broached the subject with Pascal, but you can't believe he'd let you go away for two years!"

"I can't oblige him to get engaged to me!" said Andrée, sounding agitated. "He asked me to be patient, he said he needed time to understand himself; I'm not going to throw myself at his feet, crying, 'Let's get engaged!'"

"You won't throw yourself at his feet: you'll explain the situation."

"That's the same as backing him into a corner."

"It's not your fault! There's nothing else you can do!"

She resisted for a long time, but I finally convinced her to talk to Pascal. She refused only to tell him what was happening in a letter; she told her mother she would have a conversation with him as soon as she got back. Madame Gallard acquiesced. She smiled a lot those days; perhaps she was thinking: "That's two daughters married off!" She behaved almost kindly toward me; and often, when she was arranging Andrée's pillows, or helping her switch on a reading light, something in her eyes reminded me of the photograph of her as a young girl.

Andrée had told Pascal, in a playful tone of voice, how she had hurt herself; she received two worried letters from him. He said that she needed someone responsible to watch over her, and other things that she didn't tell me; but I understood that she no longer doubted his feelings. Rest and sleep brought the color back to her face, and she even put on a little weight: never had I seen her look so radiant as the day she could finally get out of bed.

She limped a little, walked with difficulty. Monsieur Gallard loaned us his Citroën for the whole day. I had rarely been in a car, and never for pleasure. So my heart was full of delight when I sat down next to Andrée and we drove down the wide road, all the windows open. We took a very straight, long road through the forest of the Landes, between the pine trees, as high as the eye could see. Andrée drove very fast: the speedometer read nearly fifty miles an hour! Despite her competent driving, I was a little nervous.

"You're not going to get us killed?" I asked.

"Definitely not!"

Andrée smiled happily. "Now I absolutely do not want to die."

"And you did before?"

"Oh, yes! Every night when I went to sleep, I wished I would never wake up. Now I pray to God that He keep me alive," she added cheerfully.

We'd turned off the main road and were slowly winding our way past the still ponds surrounded by heather; we had lunch by the sea in an empty hotel. The summer season was ending, the beaches were deserted, the villas closed. In Bayonne, we bought multicolored nougat bars for the twins; we ate one while slowly climbing up the cloisters of the cathedral. Andrée leaned against my shoulder. We talked about the cloisters in Spain and Italy where we would go for walks one day, and other countries, even farther away, where we'd travel. On the way back to the car, I pointed to her bandaged foot: "I'll never understand how you had the courage!"

"You would have too if you'd felt as harassed as I did." She touched her temple. "I ended up getting the most unbearable headaches."

"And you don't anymore?"

"Much less often. I must admit that during that time when I couldn't sleep at night, I was having too much caffeine and amphetamines."

"You're not going to start that up again?"

"No. When we return, I'll have a difficult time for two weeks, until Malou's wedding; but now I'm stronger."

We took a small road that followed the Adour River to get back to the forest. In spite of everything, Madame Gallard had arranged for Andrée to do an errand: she had to deliver some baby clothes knitted by Madame Rivière de Bonneuil to a young farmer's wife who was expecting. Andrée stopped the car in front of a pretty country cottage, in the middle of a clearing surrounded by pine trees.

I was used to the tenant farms of Sadernac, the piles of fertilizer, the streams of manure, so the elegance of this farm hidden in the forest surprised me. The young woman offered us a glass of rosé wine that her father-in-law made himself; she opened the armoire to show off her embroidered sheets: they smelled of lavender and sweet clover. A ten-month-old baby was laughing in a wicker basket, and Andrée was entertaining him with the gold medals on her necklace: she had always loved children.

"He's very alert for his age!" said Andrée.

When she spoke, common sayings lost their banality, because her voice and the smile in her eyes were sincere.

"This one doesn't sleep either," the young woman said cheerfully, placing her hand on her stomach.

She had dark hair and olive skin, like Andrée; she had the same build, rather short legs, but a gracious bearing despite her advanced stage of pregnancy. "When Andrée is expecting a child," I thought, "she'll look just like this." For the first time, I imagined Andrée married and a mother without feeling annoyed. She would have beautiful, glistening furniture all around her, like this; everyone would feel good in her home. But she wouldn't spend hours polishing the brass and copper, or covering pots of jam with waxed paper; she would play her violin, and I was secretly convinced that she would write books: she had always loved books and writing so much.

"Happiness suits her so well!" I thought as she and the young woman talked about the baby soon to be born, and the one who was teething.

"This has been a wonderful day!" I said when, an hour later, the car stopped in front of the enormous zinnias.

"Yes," said Andrée.

I was sure that she too had been thinking of the future.

THE GALLARDS RETURNED to Paris before me, because of Malou's wedding. As soon as I arrived, I called Andrée, and we agreed to meet the next day; she seemed eager to hang up, and I didn't like chatting with her without seeing her face. I didn't ask her any questions.

I waited for her in the Champs-Élysées gardens, opposite the statue of Alphonse Daudet. She arrived a little late, and I could see right away that something was wrong: she sat down next to me without even trying to smile.

"Is everything all right?" I asked anxiously.

"No," she said. "Pascal doesn't want to," she added in an expressionless tone of voice.

"What doesn't he want?"

"To get engaged. Not now."

"So?"

"So Mama is packing me off to Cambridge as soon as the wedding is over."

"But that's absurd!" I said. "It's impossible! Pascal can't let you go away!"

"He says we'll write to each other, that he'll try to come sometime, that two years isn't that long," said Andrée in a voice devoid of emotion. She sounded like she was reciting a catechism she didn't believe in.

"But why?" I said.

Normally, when Andrée told me about a conversation, it was with such clarity that I felt as if I'd heard it with my own ears; this time, she gave me a depressing, vague account. Pascal had seemed moved when he saw her again; he'd told her he loved her, but when the word "engagement" came up, his face had changed. No! he'd said quickly, no! Never would his father allow him to get engaged so young. After all the sacrifices he had made for Pascal, Monsieur Blondel had a right to expect his son to dedicate himself body and soul to studying for his academic competitive exam: an engagement would seem frivolous. I knew that Pascal respected his father a great deal, and I could understand that his initial reaction would be a fear of causing him pain; but when he learned that Madame Gallard would not give in, how could that not take priority over his father's wishes?

"Did he understand how unhappy you felt at the idea of leaving?"

"I don't know."

"Did you tell him?"

"A little."

"You should have persisted. I'm sure you didn't really try to discuss it."

"He looked so harassed," said Andrée. "I know what it's like to feel harassed!"

Her voice trembled, and I understood she had barely listened to Pascal's argument, which she hadn't tried to refute.

"There's still time to fight," I said.

"Do I have to spend my life fighting with the people I love?"

She spoke with such anger that I did not insist.

"What if Pascal explained things to your mother?" I ventured.

"I suggested that to Mama. That wasn't enough for her. She said that if Pascal seriously intended to marry me, he would introduce me to his family; since he refuses, the only thing left to do is break things off. Mama said something really strange," said Andrée.

She paused for a moment, lost in thought. "She said: 'I know you very well; you're my daughter, my flesh and blood. You're not strong enough for me to allow you to be exposed to temptation; if you gave in, your sins would fall back on me, and I would deserve it.'"

She looked at me as if she were hoping I could help

her grasp the hidden meaning of those words; but for the moment, I couldn't give a damn about Madame Gallard's inner crises. Andrée's resignation irritated me.

"What if you refused to leave?"

"Refused? How?"

"They can't force you onto a boat."

"I could lock myself in my room and go on a hunger strike," said Andrée. "Then what? Mama would go and explain everything to Pascal's father . . ."

Andrée hid her head in her hands. "I don't want to think of Mama as an enemy! That's horrible!"

"I'll speak to Pascal," I said firmly. "You didn't know how to talk to him."

"You won't get anywhere."

"Let me try."

"Try, but you won't get anywhere."

Andrée stared hard at the statue of Alphonse Daudet, but her eyes were fixed on something other than that sad-looking marble.

"God is against me," she said.

I shuddered at that blasphemy, as if I were a believer.

"Pascal would say that you are blaspheming," I said. "If God exists, He isn't against anyone."

"How can we know? Who can understand what God is?" She shrugged. "Oh! Perhaps He's reserving a lovely spot in His heaven for me: but here on earth, he hates me.

And yet," she added in a passionate tone of voice, "there are people in heaven who were happy in this world!"

Suddenly, she started to cry. "I don't want to go away! Two years far away from Pascal, from Mama, from you: I don't have the strength to bear it!"

Never, even at the time when she broke off with Bernard, had I ever seen Andrée cry. I wanted to take her hand, make some gesture, but I remained a prisoner of our harsh past and did not move. I thought about those two hours she'd spent on the roof of the château at Béthary wondering if she should jump: there was the same darkness inside her now.

"Andrée," I said, "you're not going away: it's impossible for me not to convince Pascal."

She dried her eyes, looked at her watch, and stood up.

"It won't do any good," she said again.

I was sure of the opposite. When I called Pascal that evening, his voice was friendly and cheerful. He loved Andrée, and he could be reasoned with. Andrée had failed because she had assumed she would lose. I wanted to win, and I'd bring home the prize.

Pascal was waiting for me outside the Luxembourg Gardens: he always arrived first when we met. I sat down, and we remarked what a beautiful day it was. Around the ornamental lake where little sailboats floated on the water, the flower beds looked delicately embroidered with petit point; their well-ordered design, the clearness of the sky, everything confirmed my certainty. It was good sense, it was the truth that was about to be spoken through my words; Pascal would be obliged to yield. I attacked.

"I saw Andrée yesterday afternoon."

Pascal looked at me with an expression of understanding. "I also wanted to talk to you about Andrée. Sylvie, you have to help me."

Those were the exact words Madame Gallard had said to me in the past.

"No!" I said. "I won't help you to persuade Andrée to go to England. She mustn't go away! She didn't tell you how horrifying the idea was to her, but I know."

"She did tell me," said Pascal, "and that's why I'm asking you to help me: she must understand that there's nothing tragic about a two-year separation."

"To her, it is tragic," I said. "It's not just you she's leaving: it's her entire life. Never have I seen her so unhappy," I added fervently. "You can't inflict that on her!"

"You know Andrée," said Pascal. "You know very well that she always starts out by taking things too much to heart. Afterward, she finds some equilibrium." He continued, "If Andrée leaves willingly, sure of my love and confident about the future, the separation won't be so terrible!"

"How do you expect her to be sure of you, confident about everything, if you let her go!" I said. I looked at Pascal in dismay. "In the end, whether she is perfectly happy or horribly miserable depends on you; and you've chosen her unhappiness!"

"Oh! You have the gift of simplification," said Pascal. He picked up a kind of hula-hoop that a little girl had just thrown at his legs and quickly rolled it back to her. "Happiness, unhappiness, they're above all a question of one's tendencies."

"When it comes to Andrée's current tendencies," I said, "she'll spend all her days crying. Her heart is not as rational as yours," I added with irritation. "When she loves people, she needs to see them."

"Why must people be illogical based on the pretext of loving?" said Pascal. "I hate those romantic prejudices." He shrugged. "Physical presence is not that important, in the literal sense. Or maybe it's really too important."

"Perhaps Andrée is romantic, perhaps she's wrong, but if you love her, you must try to understand her. You won't change her with logical arguments."

I looked nervously at the flower beds of heliotrope and sage. Suddenly, I thought: "I won't change Pascal with logical arguments."

"Why are you so afraid to talk to your father?" I asked.

"It's not fear," said Pascal.

"What is it then?"

"I explained it to Andrée."

"She didn't understand a thing."

"You'd have to know my father and understand my relationship with him," said Pascal. "Sylvie, you know that I love Andrée," he continued, looking at me reproachfully, "don't you?"

"I know that you're making her miserable to spare your father the slightest trouble. Well, he must know that you're going to get married one of these days!" I said impatiently.

"He'd find it absurd if I got engaged so young; he'd think very badly of Andrée, and he'd lose all his respect for me." Pascal again looked straight at me. "Believe me! I do love Andrée. My reasons must be very serious to refuse what she's asked of me."

"I can't see any serious reasons," I said.

Pascal was searching for the right words and made a gesture of helplessness.

"My father is old, he's tired, it's sad to grow old!" he said in a voice filled with emotion.

"At least try to explain the situation to him! Make him understand that Andrée won't be able to bear being sent into exile."

"He'd say that people can bear anything," said Pascal. "He had to bear many things himself, you know. I'm certain that he would think the separation was desirable."

"But why?" I asked.

I could sense a stubbornness in Pascal that was beginning to frighten me. Yet there was only one sky above our heads, one single truth. I had an idea: "Have you spoken to your sister?"

"My sister? No. Why?"

"Talk to her. Maybe she could find a way to put things to your father."

Pascal sat silent for a moment.

"My sister would be even more upset than my father if I got engaged," he said.

I pictured Emma, her large forehead, her navy-blue dress with its white embroidered collar, and the possessive way she had when speaking to Pascal.

Of course. Emma was not an ally.

"Ah!" I said. "So it's Emma you're afraid of?"

"Why do you refuse to understand?" said Pascal. "I don't want to hurt my father or Emma after everything they've meant to me: that seems normal to me."

"Emma isn't still counting on you becoming a priest?"

"No." He hesitated. "It's no fun being old; and it's no fun living with an old person either. When I'm no longer there, the house will be sad for my sister."

Yes, I understood Emma's point of view better than Monsieur Blondel's. I wondered if, in truth, it was not especially because of her that Pascal wanted to keep his love a secret.

"They'll have to resign themselves to you leaving some-day!" I said.

"All I'm asking of Andrée is that she be patient for two years," said Pascal. "Then my father will find it normal that I'm thinking of getting married, and Emma will gradually get used to the idea. Today it would break their hearts."

"But leaving will break Andrée's heart. If someone has to suffer, why must it be her?"

"Andrée and I have our whole life ahead of us and the certainty that we will be happy later on: we can surely sacrifice ourselves for a while for those who have nothing," said Pascal, sounding slightly annoyed.

"She will suffer more than you," I said, looking at Pascal with hostility. "She's young, yes, which means that she has fire in her blood, she wants to live . . ."

Pascal nodded. "That's also a reason why it's undoubtedly preferable that we separate," he said.

I was taken aback.

"I don't understand," I said.

"Sylvie, in certain ways, you're immature for your age," he said in a tone of voice I'd heard Father Dominique use in the past when hearing my confession. "And you're not a believer: there are issues that you're unaware of."

"For example?"

"The intimacy of being engaged is not easy for Christians. Andrée is a real woman, a woman of flesh and blood. Even if we didn't give in to temptation, we would always be aware of it: that type of obsession is a sin in itself."

I felt myself blush. I hadn't anticipated that argument, and it repulsed me to imagine it.

"Since Andrée is prepared to take that risk," I said, "it's not up to you to decide for her."

"But it is; it's up to me to protect her from herself. Andrée is so generous that she would damn herself out of love."

"Poor Andrée! Everyone wants to save her. And she wants so much to have a bit of happiness on this earth!"

"Andrée feels sin more than I do," said Pascal. "I've seen her eat herself up with remorse over an innocent, childish relationship. If our relationship became troubling in any way, she'd never forgive herself."

I felt I was losing the argument; my anxiety made me stronger.

"Pascal," I said. "Listen to me. I just spent a month with Andrée: she's at the end of her tether. Physically, she's a little better, but she'll lose her appetite again, won't sleep, and will end up making herself ill. She can't take any more emotionally. Can you imagine what her state of mind must have been to cut her own foot with an ax?"

In one long speech, I summed up what Andrée's life had been like for the past five years. The heartbreak of ending her relationship with Bernard, her disappointment in discovering the truth about the world she lived in, the battle against her mother to have the right to behave according to her feelings and her conscience; all her victories were poisoned by remorse, and even the slightest feeling of desire caused her to suspect she was sinning. The longer I talked, the more I could imagine the depths of despair that Andrée had never revealed to me, but which some of her words had made me sense. I was afraid, and it seemed to me that Pascal should be frightened as well.

"Every night for the past five years, she's wanted to die," I said. "And the other day, she was so depressed that she said, 'God is against me!'"

Pascal shook his head; his face had not changed.

"I know Andrée as well as you do," he said, "and even better, because I can understand her in ways that are out of bounds to you. Much has been asked of her. But what you don't know is that God grants as many blessings as trials. Andrée has joys and consolations that you cannot imagine."

I'd lost. I quickly walked away from Pascal, head down, beneath the deceitful sky. Other arguments came to mind: they would have been of no use. It was strange. We'd had hundreds of discussions, and one of us had always convinced the other. Today something quite real had been at stake, and all logic fell apart in the face of the stubborn beliefs we held inside. During the days that followed, I often questioned myself about the true reasons behind Pascal's behavior. Was it his father or Emma who intimidated him? Did he actually believe in all those stories about temptation and sin? Or was all that nothing but a pretext? Was he repulsed by the idea of beginning to commit himself to the life of an adult? He had always imagined the future with apprehension. Oh! There would have been no problem if Madame Gallard hadn't thought of an engagement. Pascal would have calmly seen Andrée for two years; he would have become sure of their love; he would have gotten used to the idea of becoming a man. I was no less annoyed by his stubbornness because of all that. I blamed Madame Gallard, Pascal, and myself as well, because too many things about Andrée remained unclear to me, and because I couldn't really help her.

Three days passed before Andrée could find time to see me again; we arranged to meet at the tea shop at Au Printemps. All around me, women wearing perfume ate cakes and talked about the cost of living. Since the day she was born, Andrée was destined to be like them: but she wasn't. I wondered what words I would find to say to her: I hadn't even been able to find any to console myself.

Andrée walked quickly over to me. "I'm late!"

"That doesn't matter at all."

She was often late, not because she had no scruples but because she was torn between conflicting scruples.

"I'm sorry we had to meet here," she said, "but I have so little time." She put her handbag and a collection of samples on the table. "I've already been to four department stores!"

"What a job!" I said.

I knew the routine. When the younger Gallards needed a coat or a dress, Andrée would make the rounds of the best department stores and a few specialist boutiques: she would then return with samples, and after a family consultation, Madame Gallard would choose one fabric, taking into account its quality and price. This time, it was about having wedding outfits made, so it was a serious decision.

"But your parents are hardly short of money," I said impatiently.

"No, but they think that money is not meant to be wasted," said Andrée.

It wouldn't have been a waste, I thought, to spare Andrée the fatigue and boredom of such complicated purchases. She had yellowish dark circles under her eyes, her makeup clashed harshly with her pale skin. Nevertheless, to my great astonishment, she smiled.

"I think that the twins would look adorable in this blue silk."

I agreed with disinterest.

"You look tired," I said.

"The big department stores always give me a headache; I'll take some aspirin."

She ordered a glass of water and some tea.

"You should see a doctor: you get headaches too often."

"Oh! They're migraines; they come and go, I'm used to

it," said Andrée as she dissolved two aspirins in a glass of water. She smiled and drank it.

"Pascal told me about your conversation," she said. "He was a little upset because he got the impression that you were judging him very harshly." She gave me a serious look. "You mustn't!"

"I don't think he's bad," I said.

I had no other choice. Since Andrée had to leave, it was better that she trusted Pascal.

"It's true that I always exaggerate things," she said. "I think I have no strength left; but people always do."

She was nervously closing and opening her fingers, but her face was calm.

"All my unhappiness is because I don't have enough faith," she added. "I must have faith in Mama, in Pascal, in God: then I'll be able to feel they don't hate each other and don't mean me any harm."

She seemed to be talking to herself rather than to me, which was not what she normally did.

"Yes," I said. "You know that Pascal loves you and that in the end, you'll get married, so two years isn't all that long . . ."

"It's better if I go away," she said. "They're right, and I know that very well. I know very well that yielding to the flesh is a sin: I must avoid the temptations of the flesh. We must be brave enough to face the facts," Andrée added.

I said nothing, then asked, "Will you be free over there? Will you have time for yourself?"

"I'll take a few classes and I'll have a lot of time," said Andrée. She took a sip of tea; her hands had calmed down. "In that respect, my trip to England is a good opportunity; if I stayed in Paris, I would have a horrible life. In Cambridge, I'll be able to breathe."

"You must eat and sleep," I said.

"Don't worry; I'll be reasonable. But I want to work," said Andrée, her voice animated. "I'll read the English poets, there are some beautiful ones. I might try to translate something. And I'd especially like to study the English novel. I think there are many things to be said about the novel, things that have never been said." She smiled. "My ideas are still a little vague, but I've had lots of ideas recently."

"I'd love for you to tell me about them."

"And I want to talk about them with you." Andrée finished her tea. "Next time, I'll arrange to have more time. I apologize for having put you out for five minutes; I just wanted to tell you that you don't have to worry about me anymore. I've understood that things are exactly as they should be."

I left the tearoom with her and said goodbye at the candy counter. She gave me a big, encouraging smile:

"I'll call you. See you soon!"

I **LEARNED** about the events that followed directly from Pascal. I made him tell me about what happened so often and in such detail that my mind can barely distinguish it from my personal memories. It was two days later, late in the afternoon. Monsieur Blondel was correcting homework in his office; Emma was peeling vegetables. Pascal wasn't home yet. The doorbell rang. Emma dried her hands and went to open the door. She found herself facing a young girl with dark hair, properly dressed in a gray suit, but wearing no hat, which, at the time, was completely unusual.

"I'd like to speak to Monsieur Blondel," said Andrée.

Emma thought she was one of her father's former students and showed Andrée into the office. Monsieur Blondel looked in surprise at this young stranger walking toward him, holding out her hand.

"Hello, Monsieur. I'm Andrée Gallard."

"Excuse me," he said, shaking her hand, "but I don't remember you . . ."

She sat down and casually crossed her legs. "Pascal didn't tell you about me?"

"Oh! So you're a friend of Pascal's?" said Monsieur Blondel.

"Not a friend," she said, looking around her. "He isn't home?"

"No . . ."

"Where is he?" she asked, sounding worried. "Is he already in heaven?"

Monsieur Blondel looked at her closely: her cheeks were bright red; it was obvious she had a fever.

"He'll be home very soon," he said.

"Never mind. You're the one I came to see," said Andrée.

She was shivering.

"Are you looking at me to see if I have the mark of sin on my face? I swear to you that I am not a sinner; I've always fought," she said passionately, "always."

"You seem like a very nice young lady," stammered Monsieur Blondel, who was beginning to feel concerned; and to make matters worse, he was a little deaf.

"I'm not a saint," she said, wiping her forehead with her hand. "I'm not a saint, but I won't hurt Pascal. I'm begging you: don't force me to go away!"

"Go away? But where?"

"So you don't know: my mother is going to send me to England if you force me to leave."

"I'm not forcing you," said Monsieur Blondel. "There's been some misunderstanding." The word consoled him. "A misunderstanding," he said again.

"I know how to manage a household," said Andrée. "Pascal will want for nothing. And I'm not a social butterfly. If I had a little time to play my violin and to see Sylvie, I'd ask for nothing more."

She looked at Monsieur Blondel anxiously. "Don't you think I'm being reasonable?"

"Completely reasonable."

"Well then, why are you against me?"

"My dear girl, again, I'm telling you there's been some misunderstanding," said Monsieur Blondel. "I'm not against you."

He understood nothing at all about what was going on, but he felt sorry for this young woman whose cheeks were on fire; he wanted to reassure her and had spoken with such conviction that Andrée's face relaxed.

"Really?"

"I swear to you."

"Then you won't forbid us to have children?"

"Of course not."

"Seven children would be too many," said Andrée, "there's always one problem child, of course; but three or four would be good."

"Why don't you tell me your story," said Monsieur Blondel.

"Yes," said Andrée. She thought for a moment. "You see, I told myself that I should have the strength to leave for Cambridge, I told myself I would. And this morning, when I got up, I understood that I couldn't. So I came to ask you to take pity on me."

"I'm not an enemy," said Monsieur Blondel. "Tell me everything."

She began, in a rather logical way. Pascal heard her voice through the door and was stunned.

"Andrée!" he said reproachfully as he came into the room. But his father gestured to him.

"Mademoiselle Gallard needed to speak to me, and I'm very happy to have met her," he said. "But she's very tired; she has a fever. You'll take her back to her mother."

Pascal went over to Andrée and took her hand.

"Yes," he said, "you do have a fever."

"It's nothing. I'm happy: your father doesn't hate me!"

Pascal stroked Andrée's hair. "Wait here, I'll call a taxi."

His father followed him out to the adjoining room and told him about Andrée's visit.

"Why didn't you tell me what was going on?" he asked reproachfully.

"I was certainly wrong not to," said Pascal.

He suddenly felt something unknown, disturbing, unbearable rising in his throat. Andrée had closed her eyes; they waited for the taxi in silence. He took her arm and led her down the stairs. In the car, she rested her head against his shoulder.

"Pascal, why have you never kissed me?"

He kissed her.

Pascal briefly explained everything to Madame Gallard; they sat down together at the end of Andrée's bed. "You won't go away, everything's arranged," said Madame Gallard.

Andrée smiled. "We have to order some champagne," she said.

And then she became delirious. The doctor prescribed tranquilizers; he talked about meningitis, encephalitis, but made no firm diagnosis.

A telegram from Madame Gallard informed me that Andrée had been delirious all night. The doctors said she had to be put in isolation, and she was taken to the private hospital in Saint-Germain-en-Laye, where they tried everything to bring down her fever. She spent three days alone with a nurse.

"I want Pascal, Sylvie, my violin, and some champagne," she said again and again, rambling. The fever didn't come down.

Madame Gallard stayed with her on the fourth night; in the morning, Andrée recognized her.

"Am I going to die?" she asked. "I can't die before the wedding: the little ones will look so adorable in that blue silk!"

She was so weak that she could barely speak. She said the same thing several times: "I'm going to ruin the celebration! I ruin everything! I've never given you anything but trouble!"

Later on, she squeezed her mother's hands.

"Don't be sad," she said. "There's a problem child in every family: and that's me."

She may have said other things, but Madame Gallard did not repeat them to Pascal. When I called the hospital around ten o'clock, they told me, "It's over." The doctors had never made a diagnosis.

I saw Andrée in the hospital's chapel, laid out amid a row of candles and flowers. She was wearing one of her long nightdresses made of coarse cotton. Her hair had grown; it fell in straight locks around her yellowish face, so thin that you could barely make out her features. Her hands, with their long, pale claws, were crossed over a crucifix, and looked as brittle as an old mummy's.

She was buried in the little cemetery at Béthary, amid the dust of her ancestors. Madame Gallard was sobbing. "We were only the instruments of God," Monsieur Gallard said to her. The grave was covered in white flowers.

In some strange way, I understood that Andrée had died, suffocated by that whiteness. Before leaving to catch my train, I placed three red roses on top of those pristine flowers.

AFTERWORD

BY SYLVIE LE BON DE BEAUVOIR

A young brunette with short hair sits down beside Simone de Beauvoir, age nine, then a student at the Catholic Adeline Désir School. She is Élisabeth Lacoin, called Zaza, and only a few days older than Simone. Unaffected, funny, and bold, she is in sharp contrast to the prevailing conformism. But at the start of the following school year, Zaza is not there. Depressing and oppressive, the world is a dark place, until suddenly the latecomer arrives and with her the sun, joy, and happiness. Her lively intelligence and many talents seduce Simone; she admires her, is captivated. They compete for the top places in the class and become inseparable. Not that Simone doesn't have a happy family life with her beloved young mother, respected father, and submissive younger sister. But what has happened to the little ten-year-old girl is her first

emotional encounter: her feelings for Zaza are passionate; she venerates her, is terrified of displeasing her. In
the poignant vulnerability of childhood, she does not, of
course, understand the early manifestation of love at first
sight; it is to us, her witnesses, that it is so moving. Her
long conversations alone with Zaza are infinitely priceless
to her. Oh! Their upbringing constrains them—no obvious
familiarity, they use the formal *vous* with each other—but
despite their reserve, they speak in a way that Simone has
never spoken to anyone. What is this unknown feeling, the
feeling that, under the conventional label of "friendship,"
fills her young heart with passion, wonder, and ecstasy, if
not "love"? She understands very quickly that Zaza does
not feel the same attachment to her, nor does she suspect
Simone's intense feeling, but why should that matter given
the blossoming of love?

Zaza dies suddenly, one month before her twenty-
second birthday, on November 25, 1929, an unforeseen
catastrophe that continues to haunt Simone. For a long
time, her friend appeared in her dreams, her yellowish face
beneath a wide-brimmed pink hat, looking at her with
reproach. To counteract the void and to never forget her,
Simone's only recourse is the alchemy of literature. Four
times, in various forms—in the unpublished novels written
in her youth, in her collection entitled *Quand prime le
spirituel* (*When Things of the Spirit Come First*), in a passage

removed from the novel *Les mandarins* (*The Mandarins*), which won her the Prix Goncourt in 1954—four times the writer had already tried to bring Zaza back to life, in vain. In 1954 she tries again in a short, untitled novel that we are publishing here for the very first time. This final, fictional transposition leaves her unsatisfied but leads her, via an essential detour, to a decisive literary transformation. In 1958, she merges her autobiographical writing with the story of the life and death of Zaza into what would become *Mémoires d'une jeune fille rangée* (*Memoirs of a Dutiful Daughter*).

The finished novel, conserved by Simone despite her critical judgment of it, is of the greatest importance: confronted by a mystery, questioning intensifies and the various ways of approaching the subject increase, along with the possible perspectives and clarifications. And Zaza's death remains, in part, a mystery. The two writings of 1954 and 1958 that shed light on it do not exactly coincide. It is in this novel that, for the first time, the theme of their great friendship takes pride of place. Those enigmatic friendships, which, like love, caused Montaigne to remark about the relationship between himself and La Boétie: "Because it was him, because it was me."* Standing beside Andrée,

---

* Montaigne had an intense relationship with the poet Étienne de La Boétie, who, like Zaza, died suddenly, at the age of thirty-three. [Trans.]

the literary incarnation of Zaza, is a narrator who says "I": her friend Sylvie. The two "inseparable" friends are reunited, in the novel as in life, to face what had happened, but it is Sylvie who, through the prism of her friendship, recounts the events, using a contrasting technique to reveal the abiding ambiguity.

The choice of fiction implied various transpositions and modifications necessary to decipher. The last names of the characters, the places, and the family situations differ from reality: Élisabeth Lacoin is Andrée Gallard and Simone de Beauvoir becomes Sylvie Lepage. The Gallard family—the Mabilles in *Mémoires d'une jeune fille rangée*—has seven children, only one of whom is a boy. The Lacoins had nine children, six girls and three boys. Simone had only one sister, while her alias, Sylvie, has two. The Adélaïde School is easily recognizable as the famous Désir School, located on the Rue Jacob in the Saint-Germain-des-Prés area of Paris. It was there that their teachers christened the two girls "inseparable." Since this term creates a bridge between reality and fiction, it is used as the title of this work. Maurice Merleau-Ponty* becomes Pascal Blondel (Pradelle in the *Mémoires*), and has a sister who bears no resemblance to Emma in the novel. The Meyrignac estate

---

* Maurice Merleau-Ponty (1908–1961), French philosopher and one of the leading proponents of phenomenology in postwar France. [Trans.]

in Limousin is transformed into Sadernac, while Béthary is Gagnepan, where Simone stayed twice; it is one of the two residences of the Lacoin family in the Landes region, the other being Haubardin in Saint-Pandelon, which is where Zaza is buried.

So what caused Zaza's death?

According to cold, objective science, it was viral encephalitis. But was there a deadly cause that went much deeper, ensnared her entire existence in its net, finally weakened her, exhausted her, depressed her, and led to her madness and death? Simone would have replied that Zaza died because she was extraordinary. She was assassinated; her death was a "spiritualistic crime."

Zaza died because she tried to be herself and was convinced that such a desire was evil. She was born on December 25, 1907, into an upper-class, militant Catholic family, a family with strict traditions that required a dutiful daughter to be selfless, resigned, and malleable. Because Zaza was exceptional, she could not "adjust"—a sinister term that means fitting into a predetermined mold where a small dungeon awaits you, one among many; anything outside that dungeon will be constricted, crushed, thrown away like trash. Zaza could not fit the prototype; her uniqueness was destroyed. Therein lay the crime, the assassination. Simone remembers with a sense of horror a Lacoin family photo at Gagnepan, each of the nine children lined up according to their age, the six girls in the same blue taffeta dress, wearing identical straw hats decorated with cornflowers. Zaza stood in the place assigned to her for all of eternity: the second of the Lacoin daughters. The young Simone violently rejected that image. No, Zaza was not as portrayed; she was "unique."

Any unexpected emergence of freedom contradicted all the family's beliefs: the group endlessly besieged her, making her the victim of "social obligations." Surrounded by a houseful of brothers and sisters, cousins, friends, and a vast extended family, tormented by chores, social events, visits, and collective outings, Zaza has not a moment to herself; she is never alone with her friend and has no control over herself; she's allowed no personal time to practice her violin or to study: the privilege of solitude is refused her. That is why summers at Gagnepan (Béthary in the novel) are hell for her. She is suffocating, she so yearns to escape the constant presence of other people—which conjures up similar types of self-mortification in certain religious orders—that she goes as far as cutting her foot with an ax to escape a particularly odious social obligation. In this milieu, it is necessary to not stand out, not exist for oneself but to exist for others: "Mama never does something for herself, she spends her life devoted to other people," she said one day of her mother. Under the continual imposition of these constricting traditions, any spirited individualism is crushed from the start. There is no worse outrage to Simone, which is what the novel wishes to bring to light: here is a scandal that could be called philosophical, as it deals with the human condition. The affirmation of the absolute value of subjectivity lies at the heart of her beliefs and her work, not the subjectivity of the individual, one person out of a cross-section of many but of unique individuality, which makes each of us "the most irreplaceable of beings," to quote Gide, the existence of our consciousness, *hic et nunc.* "Love the thing you will never see twice." An unshakable, primal conviction, and one that philosophical reflection will support: the Absolute is played out in this world, on this earth, during our sole, unique existence. It is thus understandable that Zaza was risking everything.

What were the sources of her tragedy? Several facts intermingle and converge, one of which stands out: her adoration of her mother, whose repudiation tears her apart. Zaza loved her mother passionately, but it was a jealous, unhappy kind of love. Her surge of affection clashed with a certain coldness within her mother, and her second daughter felt drowned by a mass of siblings, being one amongst so many. Madame Lacoin skillfully did not use her authority to rein in the boisterousness of her young children but held back to better ensure control over them when anything important was involved. For a daughter, the predetermined path led straight to marriage or a convent; she could not decide her fate according to her own desires or feelings. It was up to the family to arrange marriages: organizing "interviews," selecting candidates depending on ideological, religious, social, and financial interests. Marriages took place within the same social circle. At fifteen, Zaza came into conflict with these deadly rules for the first time; they put an end to her love for her cousin through an abrupt separation, and when she was twenty, for the second time they threatened to break her. Her choice of the outsider, Maurice Merleau-Ponty (Pascal Blondel in the novel), and her hope to marry him were considered transgressions that were suspicious and unacceptable in the eyes of her clan. Zaza's tragedy was that, deep within her, an ally was slyly helping the enemy: she did not have the strength to fight a holy authority she loved so much and whose sanctions were killing her. At the very moment when maternal censure was eating away at her self-confidence and love of life, she internalized that censure and almost went as far as thinking that the judge who was condemning her was right. The repression exerted by Madame Lacoin was even more paradoxical when we perceive a crack in the foundation of her conformity: when young, it seems that she herself was forced by her mother into a marriage she found repulsive.

She had to "adapt"—and this is where that atrocious word appears—so she abandoned her convictions and, after becoming an authoritarian matron, decided to reproduce the crushing cycle of events. How much frustration and resentment were hidden beneath her self-assurance?

The burden of piety, or rather "spiritualism," weighed heavily on Zaza's life. She was steeped in an atmosphere saturated in religion, born into a dynasty of militant Catholics: a father who was president of the League of Fathers of Large Families, a mother who held a prominent place in the parish of Saint Thomas d'Aquin, one brother who was a priest, and a sister who was a nun. Every year, the family went on a pilgrimage to Lourdes. What Simone denounces in what she calls spiritualism is the "whiteness," the mystification that consists of shrouding class values that are strictly earthly in the aura of the supernatural. Naturally, the charlatans are the first to be taken in. The automatic deference to what is religious justifies everything. "We were only the instruments of God," says Monsieur Gallard after the death of his daughter. Zaza was submissive because she internalized a type of Catholicism that, for most people, is nothing more than a formal, convenient practice. Her exceptional qualities once again served her poorly. Even though she could see right through the hypocrisy, lies, and egotism of the "moralism" of her social circle, whose actions and self-interested, petty thoughts constantly betrayed the spirit of the Gospels, her faith persisted, despite being shaken for a moment. But she suffered from an internal exile, an incomprehension of those close to her, from her isolation—she who was never left alone—and from existential solitude. The authenticity of her spiritual demands served only to mortify her, in the true sense of the word, and to torture her by forcing her to suffer internal contradictions. Because, to her, faith was not, as it was for so many others, a complaisant dependence on God, a means of being right, of self-justification or fleeing responsibilities but the painful questioning of a silent, obscure, hidden God. She became her own torturer, tearing herself apart: Was it necessary to obey, stultify herself, become submissive, self-effacing, as her mother so often told her? Or should she disobey, revolt, take credit for the gifts and talents given to her, as her friend encouraged her to do? What was God's will? What did He expect of her?

The specter of sin sapped her strength. Unlike her friend Sylvie, Andrée had been educated about sex. Madame Gallard, with a brutality verging on the sadistic, had warned her fifteen-year-old daughter about the harshness of marriage. The wedding night, she openly told her, "is a bad experience to get through." Zaza's experience contradicted that cynicism: she had known the magic of sexuality, of infatuation—the kisses exchanged with her boyfriend, Bernard, were not platonic. She mocks the foolishness of the young virgins who surround her, the hypocrisy of the self-righteous people who "whitewash," deny, or hide the surge of natural needs of a living body. Yet, on the other hand, she knows she is vulnerable to temptation, and her intense sensuality, passionate temperament, and physical love of life are poisoned by an excess of scruples: at the least feeling of desire, she suspects a sin, the sin of the flesh. Remorse, fear, and guilt overwhelm her, and this self-condemnation reinforces within her the temptation to denounce, a taste for oblivion, and troubling, self-destructive tendencies. She ends up capitulating to her mother and Pascal, who persuade her of the danger of a long engagement, and agrees to go into exile in England while all her being revolts against it. This final, ferocious constraint forced on her causes the catastrophe. Zaza died of all the contradictions that tore her apart.

I CANNOT prevent myself from recalling that each of the four parts of *Mémoires d'une jeune fille rangée* ends with these words: "Zaza," "would tell the story," "of death," "her death." Simone feels guilty because surviving, in a way, is a failing. Zaza was the ransom; she even goes as far in her unpublished notes as to describe Zaza as "the sacrificial victim" of her own escape. But for us, does her novel not fulfill the quasi-sacred mission that she entrusted to words: to fight against time, to fight against forgetfulness, to fight against death, "to justify the absolute importance of the moment, the eternity of the moment that would last forever"?

SELECTED LETTERS BETWEEN SIMONE DE BEAUVOIR AND ÉLISABETH "ZAZA" LACOIN, 1920–1929

P lease note: Mistakes in punctuation and grammar in this first letter have been retained for authenticity.

PAGES 1 AND 4 of a letter from Simone to Zaza, written as a child, aged twelve, in purple ink and signed "Your inseparable friend":

WEDNESDAY, 15 SEPTEMBER 1920

My dear Zaza,

I definitely think that my laziness is only equaled by yours; it's been two weeks since all I received was your long letter, and I still haven't brought myself to reply to you. I'm having such a good time here that I haven't found time. I've just come back from hunting; it's the third time I've been. But I haven't had any luck my uncle didn't kill anything on the days I was with him. Today he hit a partridge but it fell into a bush and not having [. . . missing words] nothing's left.

Are there blackberries in Gagnepan? In Meyrignac we have a lot, the hedges are covered in them so we're loving them. Goodbye my dear Zaza don't make me wait for your letter as long as I made you wait for mine. I kiss you with all my heart as well as your brothers and sisters and especially your goddaughter. Send my regards to Madame Lacoin and best wishes from Mama. Your inseparable friend. Simone. Hope you can read my scrawl without too much difficulty.

GAGNEPAN, 3 SEPTEMBER 1927

My dear Simone,

Your letter arrived at a moment when a few hours of talking to myself and sincere reflection had just given me much more lucidity and understanding of myself than I've had since the beginning of the vacation. I was so happy reading your letter and feeling that we were still so close to each other, while your last letter gave me the impression that you were distancing yourself a lot from me and suddenly changing direction. Forgive me, in short, for having misunderstood you. My error arose from the letter before this last one in which you stressed a great deal your search for the truth, your most recent aspiration; it's just that this conclusion is only a goal, a meaning given to your existence, I believed I saw a renunciation of everything else, an abandonment of everything that is so beautiful in our humanity. I can see that you are far from thinking of a desecration of that sort and that you are renouncing nothing of yourself; it is in that, I am convinced of it now, that true strength lies, and I think that it is necessary to attain a certain level of internal perfection where all our contradictions evaporate and our *true self* blossoms in all its glory. And that's why I liked what you expressed when you said "saving oneself entirely" which is the most beautiful human conception of existence and not very far off from "seeking your own salvation" in the Christian religion when understood in the wider sense.

[. . .] Even though you might not have said so, I could sense that you are now feeling a very great feeling of peace within you, thanks to the calmness your letter brought to me. There is nothing sweeter in the world than feeling there is someone who can completely understand you and on whose friendship you can count on absolutely.

Come as soon as you can; the 10th, if possible, would work for us, or any other date. You'll meet the de Neuvilles again, who will be here from the 8th to the 15th; so the first few days you'll find very busy, but I'm really hoping you'll stay long after they leave and that you will enjoy the peacefulness of Gagnepan as much as its hustle and bustle. I sense that my saying "have fun to forget everything" caused you to feel something like a reproach and I want to explain myself, for I have exaggerated my thought a great deal; I know from experience that there are times when nothing can distract me from myself and that having fun is then torture. Recently, in Haubardin, we organized a long excursion with friends in the Basque Country; I needed solitude then to such an extent, felt it so impossible to enjoy myself that I gashed my own foot with an axe to avoid going on that expedition. I had to lie on a chaise longue for a week and listen to words full of pity as well as outcries about my carelessness and clumsiness, but at least I had a bit of solitude and the right to not speak and not have fun.

I truly hope I won't have to cut my foot while you're visiting; on the 11th, we decided to travel twenty-five kilometers from here to the Landes to their version of the "Riding of the Bulls"* and go down to an old château where some of our cousins live. Try to be here, please. As for your train, I don't know what to say. Will you come via Bordeaux or Montauban? If it's via Montauban, we can come and get you at Riscle, which isn't far from here, so you don't have to change trains. Take whichever one you

---

* This is a reference to a traditional event in the Landes region where the animals are not hurt. The men jump on the bulls' backs and tie a ribbon to their horns. In French, it is called *la course des vaches*. [Trans.]

want, I'll come in the car any time of day or night to pick you up.

I really want to know how you're spending your vacation; if you could write to me as soon as you get this letter, I'll be able to have your news; send it to Marseille, to the P.O. Box. I am so often with you despite the distance. You know that, but I'm saying it to have the pleasure of seeing my pen write a truth that is so indisputable.

I send you much love, friendly wishes to Poupette and my regards to your parents.

Zaza

ONLY PAGES 1 AND 3 of the following letter have been conserved. The letter is written on paper with black edging, used when in mourning, as Simone's grandfather had recently died (12 May 1929 in Meyrignac). Page 3 also contains an entry from Simone de Beauvoir's journal dated 1 May.

Page 1:

(PARIS) SUNDAY, 23 JUNE 1929

Dear, dear Zaza,

How can I think of you so very much without having the desire to tell you? This evening, I feel the thirst for your presence that, as a young girl, so often made me cry out of affection. But then, I didn't dare write to tell you; now, should I stop myself from doing so, at a time when two days without you seems, ridiculously, a long absence?

It seems to me that you felt, as I did, that during these past two weeks we reached a marvelous point in our friendship; on Friday, for example, I would have given anything in the world to have time go on indefinitely between us and Rumplemeyer.

In Gagnepan as well, we had some very beautiful

days: a walk in the woods when we talked about Jacques; one night especially whose memory within me is as beautiful as it is impossible. But there still remained some sort of effort for us to reach that point, a distrust of the future, the fear of only fleeting success.

And there was your return from Berlin: the evening we went to pick up Poupette together; the next evening at *Prince Igor*—those times remain within me as magnificent as promises of things to come. Those final days contain a beauty more rare than accomplishments. From you to me, with a much clearer awareness of what you must deny yourself, and because of that very awareness, a sense of trust, a far more comfortable feeling of affection; from me to you, the certainty of being understood, the feeling that I understand you better than ever, perhaps, and surely the incomparable joy of admiring without restraint what is more totally understood than ever. If we had played at inventing a game . . .

Page 3:

. . . the signs of affection to be sure of preferring him; and that in giving to each one the place in my heart they could hold, this heart remains entirely his.

I often feel that way, almost in spite of myself, for I have willingly forbidden myself to see him again, to question myself about him; his presence, whatever it brings me, whether it disappoints me or fulfills me, is too heavy for me to bear alone—even though I know it will fulfill me.

Good night, dear Zaza
Your Simone

PS: I wanted in this letter to tell you of my affection for you and also to give you proof of the infinite faith I have in you. Re-reading it, I can see that it contains only reticence. This reticence will be more easily broken down by speaking than by writing.

But as for what concerns me, why lie again to myself, to us. Here I have recopied for you, still intact in what I deem ridiculous this evening, a few passages of my notes to which I still believe today with all my heart.

ENTRY FROM Simone de Beauvoir's journal dated 1 May:

~~SATURDAY, 26 JANUARY~~   1 MAY

But knowing nothing about the other person, will that count as nothing to me? So splendidly found once more, unique! . . . Oh! This trick of my heart that wants to diminish you in order to suffer less. Is it suffering? Despite everything, I know that you are so close to me, and that it is towards me, not towards someone else, that you are coming; but how far away is that radiant domain . . .

You are such an extraordinary being, Jacques! Extraordinary . . .

Why always not dare to admit what I know, and be mistrustful of the judgment of my heart? You are an extraordinary being, the only one in whom I have felt incomparable in terms of talent, success, intelligence, genius, the only one who takes me beyond peace, beyond joy . . .

LETTER FROM Zaza to Simone. She talks about her feelings for Merleau-Ponty.

THURSDAY EVENING, 10 OCTOBER 1929

My dear Simone,

I am not writing as Gandillac* likes doing to excuse myself for having been so gloomy yesterday, despite the vermouth and the comforting welcome at the "Bar Sélection."† I'm sure you understood that I was still reeling from the telegram I got the day before. It came at a very bad time. If P. [Merleau-Ponty] could have imagined the emotions I felt about our meeting on Thursday, I think he would not have postponed it. But it's very good that he didn't know; I like what he has done a lot and it wasn't bad for me to see the extent to which my discouragement could grow when I remain absolutely alone in resisting

---

* Maurice de Gandillac (1906–2006) was a philosopher born in French Algeria. He was a professor of philosophy at the Sorbonne (1946) and supervised Foucault and Derrida, among others. [Trans.]

† The "Bar Sélection" was the name given to the room that Simone de Beauvoir rented from her grandmother in September 1929, located at 91 Avenue Denfert. It was the first time she lived independently.

my bitter thoughts and the morose warnings that Mama feels necessary to give me. The saddest thing is to not be able to communicate with him. I didn't dare send him a note at Rue de la Tour. If you had been alone yesterday, I would have written him a few lines with your illegible handwriting on the envelope. It would be very kind of you if you could send him a telegram right away telling him what he already knows, I hope: that I am very close to him in suffering as in joy, but especially that he can write to me at home as much as he likes. He should not hesitate to do so, because if it isn't possible that I see him, and very soon, I will desperately need at least a word from him. Moreover, he shouldn't fear my cheerfulness now. Even if I talked to him about us, it would be rather seriously. Assuming that his presence liberates me and gives me the happy reassurance that I had on Tuesday while chatting with you in the courtyard of the Lycée Fénelon, there remains in life far too many sad things we can talk about when you feel you are in mourning. The people I love should not worry, I'm not running away from them. I feel myself tied to this world at the moment, and even to my own life, as I never have before. And I care a lot about you, Simone, distinguished and amoral woman, I care with all my heart.

Zaza

PARIS, MONDAY, 4 NOVEMBER 1929

My dear Simone,

I saw P. [Merleau-Ponty] on Saturday, his brother is leaving this very day for Togo; until the end of the week, he'll be busy with classes or the desire to keep his mother company for a while as she is finding this separation so difficult. We would be very, very happy to meet you on Saturday at the "Bar Sélection" and to see you, whom I always miss, in your delightful grey dress. I know that our little friends are going out together on Saturday, why not bring them around to see us, do they feel such a great revulsion at seeing us, are you afraid that we'll tear each other apart? As for me, I am eager to meet Sartre as soon as possible, I found the letter you read me infinitely pleasing, and the poem beautiful, which, despite its awkwardness, made me think a lot. Between now and Saturday, for family reasons that would be too long to explain, I won't be able to see you alone as I had hoped. Wait a little.

I think of you always and love you with all my heart.

Zaza

NOTE: This is the last letter from Simone de Beauvoir to Zaza, written on 13 November 1929; Zaza was already very ill and probably unable to read it. In it is the final use of the expression "My inseparable friend." Zaza died on 25 November.

WEDNESDAY (13 NOVEMBER 1929)

Dear Zaza,

I'm counting on you for Sunday at 5 o'clock. You'll see Sartre who is on leave.* I'd really like to see you before then. What if we went to the Salon d'Automne† on Friday from 2:00–4:00 or Saturday around the same time? If you can, send me a note right away saying where we should meet. I'm going to try to see Merleau-Ponty one of these days when he finishes classes. In any case, send him my most affectionate regards if you see him before I do.

I hope that all the problems you told me about the other day are over. I was happy, so happy about

---

* Sartre's military service had just begun.
† The Salon d'Automne is an annual art exhibition held in Paris. [Trans.]

the times we spent together, my very dear Zaza. I'm still going to the B.N.,* are you going to come too?

I find happiness on every page, happiness in bigger and bigger writing. And I am closer to you now than ever before, my dear past, dear present, my dear inseparable friend. Lots of love, Zaza dearest.

S. de Beauvoir

---

* The Bibliothèque Nationale (National Library). [Trans.]

ACKNOWLEDGMENTS

WITH THANKS to Sylvie Le Bon de Beauvoir and the Association Élisabeth Lacoin for their gracious collaboration.